Dear Brio Girl,

Ever made a promise you didn't keep? If so, you'll easily relate to Hannah, who breaks a promise not only to herself but to God as well. And when her promise involves the opposite sex . . . well, everything becomes blurry—God, guys, friends, even her deepest beliefs. In the midst of the confusion, however, Hannah discovers something about God that changes her life forever. Guess what—it could change yours, too!

Your Friend,

Susie Shellenberger,
BRIO Editor
www.briomag.com

BRIO GIRLS®

from Focus on the Family®
and
Tyndale House Publishers, Inc.

---

1. *Stuck in the Sky*
2. *Fast Forward to Normal*
3. *Opportunity Knocks Twice*
4. *Double Exposure*
5. *Good-bye to All That*
6. *Grasping at Moonbeams*
7. *Croutons for Breakfast*
8. *No Lifeguard on Duty*
9. *Dragonfly on My Shoulder*
10. *Going Crazy Till Wednesday*
11. *When Stars Fall*
12. *Bad Girl Days*

brio girls™

REAL Faith MEETS REAL Life℠

Solana Becca Jacie Tyler

Double Exposure

Created by

LISSA HALLS JOHNSON

WRITTEN BY KATHY WIERENGA BUCHANAN

TYNDALE

Tyndale House Publishers, inc.
Wheaton, Illinois

A Focus on the Family book published by
Tyndale House Publishers, Inc., Wheaton, Illinois 60189; First printing, 2005
Previously published by Bethany House under the same ISBN.

Cover design by Lookout Design Group, Inc.
Editor: Lissa Halls Johnson

Library of Congress Cataloging-in-Publication Data

Wierenga, Kathy.
Double exposure / created by Lissa Halls Johnson ; written by Kathy Wierenga.
p. cm. — (Brio girls)
Summary: In public school after eleven years of home schooling, sixteen-year-old Hannah struggles to reconcile her religious convictions about courtship with her growing attraction to a boy.
ISBN 1-56179-954-8
[1. Courtship—Fiction. 2. Dating (Social customs)—Fiction. 3. Christian life—Fiction. 4. High schools—Fiction. 5. Schools—Fiction.] I. Johnson, Lissa Halls, 1955- II. Title. III. Series.

PZ7.W63583 Do 2002
[Fic]—dc21 2001006281

Printed in the United States of America

11 10 09 08 07 06 05
9 8 7 6 5 4 3 2 1

For Rob.
May your heart always run free—
and spur others on to do the same.

KATHY WIERENGA BUCHANAN resides in Colorado Springs where she loves spending time with her husband, Sean, and their baby girl. She's on staff at Focus on the Family as a writer and director for the children's radio show, ADVENTURES IN ODYSSEY® and enjoys writing for the Brio Girls® series too. She received her Bachelor's degree from Taylor University and a Master's degree in Biblical Counseling from Colorado Christian University. Kathy is passionate about hiking the mountains, traveling around Italy and, most of all, knowing God intimately and continuing to experience His redemption in her life.

chapter 

JOURNAL

Dear God,

I received a letter from Aubrey today. It made me miss her and Deborah so much. I feel connected more to them than anybody else—they think like I do, especially about things like courtship. I feel really alone here. Even though Jacie, Becca, and Tyler are wonderful and have welcomed me as part of their group, I still feel like an outsider. We see things so differently. Like courtship. They think it's pretty odd and see nothing wrong with dating. It's strange—this is something that

I've believed in so strongly for years, and now I can't seem to make anyone understand why it's so important.

Maybe the Solana thing is another reason I feel disconnected from them. She's been their friend for years, and yet they don't do much to evangelize her. They'll talk about Christian stuff when she's around, but they're not very aggressive about sharing the gospel with her. I don't understand that.

I wonder if that's why You have me here at Stony Brook, God. I wonder if I'm supposed to show them how to evangelize and share with them how beneficial courtship is.

I want to be a good influence, God. But it's hard when I feel so alone.

● ● ●

Hannah stared over her untouched salad. "I'm dreading this class. Absolutely dreading it."

Her three friends around the cafeteria table nodded. Hannah saw their amusement behind the sympathy on their faces. Jacie's ready grin broke through her smooth, cream-with-a-touch-of-coffee complexion. "You'll survive, Hannah. Everyone does."

"I feel sorry for Ms. Bennett," Solana said. She ran her hand through her long black hair, searching for nonexistent split ends. "It's hard enough teaching a sex-ed class to a bunch of immature freshmen, but with Miss Christian Conservative in the mix—*that* would be crazy."

Becca drummed her short nails on the tabletop. "It's gonna be a lot more interesting than when we took it."

"It's a *health* class," Hannah corrected her. "I'm not even going to be there for the sex education part of it."

"How'd you get out of that?" asked Becca.

"And why would you want to?" Solana asked, her chocolate eyes wide.

"My parents requested that I go to the library instead. My parents will teach me all I need to know about . . . um . . . sex." Hannah felt her cheeks turn red. She took a bite of her sandwich.

"Whew, that's different." Jacie shook her head. "My mom *wanted* me to go to sex-ed. She figured I'd hear about sex somewhere, anyway. So we talked about what Ms. Bennett taught in class. We had some really good discussions."

Becca made a face. "My mom talked to me about sex, too. We went through this book on adolescence when I was like, 12. I was so embarrassed. We can talk more openly about it now. But it's still kind of awkward."

Hannah finished chewing and swallowed. "Even though I'm really shy when Mom talks about it, that's far better than learning about it with a bunch of people I hardly know. That's embarrassing *and* disgusting."

And I'm so glad Tyler is playing a pick-up game of basketball in the gym today. I'd be mortified if he was here.

"The girls giggle and the guys punch each other," Becca said. "What a mature discussion."

"If sex is meant to be something beautiful between two people who are committed to spending a lifetime together, then why are we talking about it around people who just cheapen it?" Hannah hesitated, realizing she must sound like she was quoting from a textbook. "We don't need to be filling our minds with thoughts that speak positively of sex in a context other than marriage." One of her favorite verses flashed through her mind. *Whatever is right, pure, good . . . think upon these things.*

"Then why are you so worried about today if the class isn't even about sex?" asked Solana, popping a ketchup-drenched fry into her mouth.

"We're talking about boy-girl relationships this week," Hannah said. "It's almost as bad as talking about sex."

"Oh yeah. I remember that part," Becca said. She perched her athletic body on the back of the cafeteria chair. "Ms. Bennett will talk about the 'emotional aspects' of relationships, like how to decide who to date—all the stuff you don't believe in."

"I still don't get it, Hannah," Solana said, flipping her long hair behind her like a whip. "*No comprendo.* You're a red-blooded 16-year-old. You might as well give up breathing."

"It's not like that," Hannah protested. "I *like* the high standards my parents have set for me." These ongoing debates about courtship and dating with Solana usually ended with Hannah reciting the top ten reasons *Why Courtship Is Best.* Today she wasn't in the mood to get into a full-blown deliberation.

"Did you ever talk about sex in homeschool?" Jacie asked.

To Jacie she said, "Yes, but not with my brothers and sisters. It was always one-on-one with my mom, not part of the curriculum we followed."

Solana sat with a french fry poised in midair. After a moment, she spoke. "But don't you ever wonder about the stuff your mom *didn't* tell you?"

"What goes into your brain comes out in your actions," quipped Hannah. "I'd rather fill my mind with more uplifting topics."

Solana's eyes shifted toward a tall, athletic boy coming through the main doors of the cafeteria. Her boy radar could pick up a romantic interest within a 200-foot radius. "Well *my* mind is filled with Marcus

McAllister." She flashed a flirtatious grin toward Marcus. "He's uplifting enough for me."

"Speaking of Marcus," Becca said. "I noticed you signed up for the ski trip next weekend."

"How could I *not* go? He's the captain of the ski team." Solana raised an eyebrow. "He'll need a personal cheering squad when he beats everyone else down the mountain."

"But you don't like to ski that much," Jacie reminded her.

"Precisely the point." Solana remained undeterred. "I need the practice."

"And I'm sure you're hoping to get some one-on-one coaching while you're there," Becca teased.

"You catch on quick," grinned Solana. "But I doubt the topic will only be skiing."

"Of course not." Becca rolled her eyes. She bent over to drape her arm around Jacie's shoulders. "However, there are others who are serious about hitting the slopes."

Jacie nodded. "I can't wait! The feel of wind in your face as you fly down the mountain, conquering a mogul run."

"The view from the top . . ." Becca said, her eyes seeing something far away.

Jacie, who was afraid of heights, shivered. "Well, maybe not the view from the top."

"The sound of the skis against powder," Becca continued. "The spray of snow on a good turn . . ."

"Sliding on your back with your skis 20 feet up the mountain after a wipeout. The feeling of ice in your underwear," Solana said. "No thanks. I intend to convince Marcus to take a break from skiing to sip hot chocolate with me by the fireplace—warm and cozy."

"Hey, guys," Tyler interrupted, trotting to the table.

"Hi, Ty," greeted Jacie. "We're talking about the ski trip."

"Cool. I'm psyched about it." He turned to Hannah. "Are you going?"

"No. I've never really skied before," replied Hannah.

"Then you have to go!" Tyler looked at the others for support. "I mean, how can you be a true Coloradoan if you don't?"

"*I'm* doing just fine at it," Solana said.

"I'm really not interested," Hannah said as the bell rang. "Besides, I have more important things to worry about right now—like this class."

"C'mon, we'll walk you to the torture chamber," volunteered Becca.

Most of the time Hannah rushed to her classes to be seated well before the bell rang. Today she held back as the five-some walked down the halls of the triangular-shaped school. Her friends waved and shouted greetings to passersby, but Hannah withdrew into her own world.

Sometimes she couldn't believe that after 11 years of homeschooling she attended a public high school. It was like being on a different planet. She had never been exposed to so many unimportant things, like what was fashionable or who was popular. No one at home or church cared about those kinds of things. After 16 years of being primarily around her family, she felt comfortable with herself and accepted.

At Stony Brook a lot of kids had expectations about the way she should look and act, even who she spent time with. Here people thought she was strange—the alien visiting from Homeschool World. And that made her more thankful than ever to have the Brio gang. At least this group of Christians saw her as a little different, but likeable, too. To most kids at Stony Brook she felt just plain weird.

"Have fun in class," smiled Becca, breaking into Hannah's thoughts.

They had reached the door to her health class too soon.

"Yeah, don't learn too much about dating," added Solana with a mischievous smirk. "We don't want you turning into a wild child."

"I still can't believe I have to do this. What kind of school has classes like this?" complained Hannah for the fifth time that day.

"A school like every other public school in the country," said Jacie, putting her hand on Hannah's arm. "Don't worry; you'll be fine."

"I'll be horribly embarrassed." Hannah's forehead creased with concern. "What else do they talk about?"

"I don't remember much," began Becca.

"The only thing I remember is that we went around the room and had to say when we started our periods and how we felt about it," Solana said.

Hannah's eyes widened. Becca and Solana erupted into laughter.

"Stop it, you guys," Jacie said. "You're scaring her."

Tyler turned to Hannah. "They're just joking. It's not that bad."

"But you're a guy!" Hannah said. "Things aren't as embarrassing to you. I can't believe your friends say stuff like that with you around."

She knew the girls were joking, but she could feel her ears turning the color of the ketchup on Solana's fries.

"I need to get to class, and so do the rest of you," said Jacie. "You're really going to be okay," she said, giving Hannah a quick hug.

I'll be okay?

She set her jaw and straightened her shoulders.

I'll be fine.

chapter 2

The group waved good-bye and set off down the hall. Hannah reached for the door and hesitated. Her stomach churned and sweat dampened her hands.

This is stupid. It's only a class.

She took two steps away from the door to let some other kids go inside. Some freshman boys shoved each other back and forth across the hallway, eliciting angry comments from those getting bumped. As Hannah moved out of the way, a bulletin board caught her eye. A bunch of different colored papers and old staples with flecks of paper still stuck underneath them covered its surface.

What am I going to do? Maybe I should go to the nurse and tell her I'm sick.

She sighed. *Sometimes it would be easier if I could lie.*

She began to read the announcements. A lunch meeting for the French club. Several flyers for the ski trip. A chess club tournament. The Winter Ball. She almost skipped over the smallest of them all.

PHOTOGRAPHER NEEDED

Photographer needed for candids, event photos
Stony Brook Times
Apply in the newspaper office

Hannah chewed her lip, ignoring the students pushing past her. *Should I?* She loved taking pictures and received many compliments on them.

She sighed again. *Okay, enough procrastinating about this class. Just do it.* She'd have to think about photography later.

Hannah took a deep breath and stepped into the classroom. Even though the others in class were only a couple years younger than she, they seemed to have the maturity level of her four-year-old brother. Guys sat on top of their desks, flicking paper wads at each other and using ratty folders as shields against the incoming ammunition. Girls watched, giggling among themselves, as though the stupid comments the boys made were incredibly funny. The cuter the boy, the harder they laughed at the not-so-funny joke.

Hannah slipped into an empty seat as far away from the action as possible, hoping no one would notice her.

It didn't work. Her 5'9" model stature announced her presence. Her perfect figure was obvious despite the long broomstick skirt and modest cream-colored blouse. A hush fell over the guys as they pointed her out to the others with their eyes. Hannah absorbed herself into a blank piece of notebook paper in front of her, ignoring their attention. She never knew what to do when others watched her. She wished she had let her golden-blond hair hang free that day so it would have covered her face, giving at least an illusion of privacy.

She used to wear her hair in a bun almost every day except when she ran. Then she wore it in a ponytail. The first time the Brio girls had met Hannah, she'd worn her hair down. And now they always nagged her to wear it down more.

"Your hair is gorgeous!" Jacie said. "Why do you always hide it in a bun?"

Hannah blushed a little. "It seems less vain."

"Do you think I'm vain when I wear my hair down?" countered Becca.

"Of course not."

"Hannah," Jacie told her, "God gave you beautiful hair. You shouldn't be ashamed of it. You should be proud of it."

Ever since that conversation, she sometimes brushed her long tresses in the morning and left them that way. Or she pulled the front back in a clip. She liked the feeling of her hair swinging across the middle of her back. It also gave her an extra layer of protection for moments like this when she didn't want others to see her face.

The petite health teacher, Ms. Bennett, burst through the door. "Good afternoon, everyone!" She glanced around the room. "It looks as though everyone is here. At least I hope so, since we don't have any desks left."

"I'll volunteer to leave if you need me to," shouted a smart aleck from the back. He must have been cute because all the girls laughed.

"That won't be necessary." Ms. Bennett smiled. She took a stack of graded assignments and began to pass them out.

Hannah looked out the window to the grounds below. A crisp wind blew across the surface of the brook that flowed through the grassy area. Hannah wished she could be out there running. She loved that time of being alone, of listening to her feet pounding the dirt of the red clay paths, surrounded by the stoic mountains—away from the gabbing of younger siblings and immature freshmen—

Ms. Bennett broke into her thoughts. "We've completed our section on nutrition, so today we'll be entering the life skills segment of the class. This week we'll be discussing dating relationships."

"Can we do homework in pairs?" called the smart aleck.

Ms. Bennett shot a stern glance at the offender, silencing him.

It always surprised Hannah how disrespectful the students in public school were toward teachers and each other. Hannah knew Solana still found it amusing that Hannah winced whenever another student cursed or said something vulgar.

Ms. Bennett perched herself on the edge of her desk and ran her hand through her short red curls.

"How many of you have had a girlfriend or boyfriend or have been out on a date?" Ms. Bennett skimmed the sea of raised hands.

"What if you have a boyfriend but you can't go anywhere alone with him yet?" asked one honest girl in the front row.

"Still counts. Even if it was back in third grade."

The class giggled.

It didn't take Hannah more than a glance to realize that she was the only one in the entire room who didn't have her hand raised. Ms. Bennett looked over in her direction and raised her eyebrows. She started to say something and then looked as though she had changed her mind.

"So most of you have had emotional connections or romantic experiences with the opposite sex, which is common for people your age. Anyone care to share any stories?"

Candid discussion filled the rest of the period, but Hannah was, once again, an outsider. She couldn't relate to embarrassing dates, first kisses, or guys who couldn't keep their hands to themselves. She spent the forty minutes alternating her intense concentration from the light fixtures to the windows to the floor tiles and back to the light fixtures again. *Things that are pure. Things that are lovely*, her mind quoted when the stories became more immodest.

"It sounds like almost all of you," Ms. Bennett's eyes met Hannah's, "have a foundation of relating romantically to the opposite sex. The rest of the week we'll be talking about how to communicate with the opposite gender, decide what kind of people you want to date, and also how to know if and when you're ready to become sexually active."

All of these ideas were foreign to Hannah. Courtship had always been a part of her life. Her circle of church families considered dating unwise—no one would talk about it in a positive way like this. Not only was courtship more biblical; it made more sense. She knew she couldn't let this discussion go by without saying anything. She prided herself in having strong convictions, and she knew she would regret it if she let this opportunity slip away. Hannah's hand shot up before she could think too much about it.

"Yes, Hannah?"

Hannah hesitated for a second. "Are we going to have any discussions about courtship?" She ignored the giggles around her.

"We're not living in a little house on a prairie," muttered a voice behind her.

Ms. Bennett gave her a blank look. "Courtship?"

"Yes, ma'am. Not dating at all. Courting with the intent to marry."

Ms. Bennett replied, choosing her words carefully. "That isn't addressed in this particular curriculum."

"It seems like that would be a logical concept to spend some time talking about since it's a healthier alternative to dating. Don't you think?"

The bell rang.

"Awww, just when it was getting interesting," said a disappointed guy on the other side of the room.

"We'll pick up here tomorrow," Ms. Bennett said. "Thanks, everyone. Have a good afternoon."

While the class filed out, Hannah lingered at her desk. When the last student disappeared through the door, she approached her teacher. "I'm sorry if I was disrespectful, Ms. Bennett. I didn't mean to be. I just don't agree with how these topics on relationships are handled." Her heart pounded, but she knew she had to pursue this.

"No need to apologize, Hannah. I understand your point. But, frankly, courtship as you described is not practical in this society."

"What do you mean?"

"Our society is based on trial and error. Discovery and learning from experience. Courtship is not applicable to the majority of our students. They're not interested—"

"They can't be interested if they haven't heard about it. They don't know there are better options than dating," Hannah insisted.

"Hannah . . ."

She could see that Ms. Bennett was searching for a way to let her down easy. *How can I make Ms. Bennett understand how important this is?* "Ms. Bennett, you've been teaching here for a while, and I know a lot of students confide in you. I would guess you've had dozens of girls in here crying on your shoulder because they gave some guy their heart, and he tore it to shreds."

"Yes, but that's a part of growing up. When a heart gets broken a few times it builds character."

"That's a high price for character, don't you think?" Hannah's heart beat faster. She couldn't believe she was talking to Ms. Bennett—an authority figure—like this. But she didn't want to stop. "Dating also encourages young women to base their identity on what some guy thinks about them and make decisions based on what will please him, instead of what might be the best thing to do or not do. That's not healthy."

The teacher gave her an amused smile. "I can tell you feel strongly about this." She took a deep breath and paused. "I have an idea. You seem to be the expert, so you can lead a discussion on courtship this Thursday."

"Really?" Inside, Hannah rejoiced over her victory. Still, her stomach churned. *This is a good thing*, she reminded herself, hoping to calm her stomach. "The whole class period?"

"I'll give you the last half of class. But," she warned, "don't use it as a platform for religious beliefs, okay?"

"Agreed."

Hannah almost skipped out of the room. *I'll take what I can get. Who knows what this could lead to?*

chapter 

"She said you could do what?" Becca asked.

The four girls lounged on facing mismatched couches at the Copperchino, their favorite coffee hangout. They often gathered there after school on cold days, and today definitely qualified. The wind howled outside, scattering a few snowflakes—scouts for an upcoming blizzard.

Solana didn't share Hannah's enthusiasm. "I can't believe it. You're going to talk about courtship at Stony Brook High? What is this world coming to?"

"I think it's an answer to prayer," said Hannah. She snuck a quick glance at Solana's reaction, but the pretty Hispanic girl remained blank-faced.

Jacie smiled. "I think it's great. Even if you don't convert anyone to courtship, it'll be good for them to hear about being more careful in relationships." She reached over and gave Hannah a side hug.

"Yeah, it is," agreed Becca. "I just can't believe it."

Hannah sat and listened to the reactions of the others. Becca and Jacie were happy for her; Solana just thought the whole thing was crazy. She was anxious to hear what Tyler would think.

She and Jacie had gotten to be better friends in the last couple months. And she loved working with Becca at the Outreach Center. It was a passion of both of theirs to help those who were less fortunate. But Solana still intimidated her. Hannah couldn't figure the girl out. She didn't know how someone could spend so much time with Christians and not be converted to the faith. Solana wasn't immoral, but she was boy-crazy. Actually, that was an understatement. She was boy-obsessed.

Of everyone in the group, Hannah felt Tyler had welcomed her the most. He seemed to appreciate her right off the bat and was a great listener. He would lock his eyes onto hers and she knew she had his complete attention. He listened when she talked about her frustrations with people and how secular the world was becoming and how the church compromised in living the truth. He was interested in her family and asked questions about them. He even came to her rescue when someone had stolen her bike wheel.

As if reading her thoughts, Becca glanced at her watch. "Where is that boy? He's late."

"Ooh, call the *Enquirer*. That's news for ya," responded Solana. "He better come *rapido*—the coffee guy can't keep his eyes off Hannah."

"Hannah," Becca said, "maybe if you pretended to be choking on something, Tyler would come running through the door."

"Of course," chimed in Solana. "His Hannah radar would go off in his head and he would race right over to rescue you."

"First stopping by the nearest phone booth to change into his super-duper-turbo boxers so he can fly here," added Becca.

Hannah started to laugh and tried to swallow at the same time. Her juice caught in her throat, throwing her into a coughing fit. Jacie handed her a glass of water. Solana didn't miss a beat. "Now we can see if the radar works."

As if on cue, Tyler entered, chilling the entire restaurant with the wind that followed him. "Are you okay, Hannah?" he asked with concern. The girls started laughing so hard they couldn't reply. Hannah kept coughing.

"So, Tyler, tell me," Becca asked. "What color are the super-duper-turbo boxers?"

Tyler shook his head. "You guys are weird," he responded. "How'd the health class go, Hannah?" Tyler directed his gaze to the willowy blonde, his blue eyes penetrating hers.

"She gets to teach a class on courtship," Jacie blurted. Then, catching herself, looked at Hannah. "Sorry, I couldn't resist."

"You're kidding! That's great! Are you excited about it?"

"Yes and no. Usually I can stand in front of anyone and say anything about my faith. But I've never presented my beliefs in front of so many people at once. I'm a little nervous," she confided.

"Oh, you'll be great. You're the perfect one to talk about courtship," insisted Tyler. "I'm gonna go grab some coffee." He turned and moved toward the counter.

Hannah sank back into the couch, watching Tyler's back as he joked around with the coffee guy. He seemed so lighthearted and yet so caring. *Maybe there's still hope. Maybe out of all my friends he'll be the one who changes his mind and chooses courtship.*

"He's looking at you again," Jacie said, nodding toward the coffee guy.

Hannah looked over at the boy behind the counter, who flicked his eyes back to Tyler. "No he's not."

"Is too," Becca said. "He's always watching you every time we come in here."

"He goes to our school, doesn't he?" Jacie asked.

"Yeah. Cute, strong, silent—just your type," Becca said. "Maybe we should ask him over—"

"Becca! Quit it!" Hannah said, grabbing Becca's arm to hold her back.

"Silent is certainly not my type," Solana said. She shook her head. "I'm never going to understand your whole deal with courtship." She took a long sip of her vanilla latte, leaving a trace of foam on her upper lip. "What's so wrong with dating? I give it two thumbs up."

Hannah always seemed to get into it with Solana. They disagreed about pretty much everything. But Solana sometimes acted like debating with her on issues was some weird kind of entertainment. Still, Hannah answered her. "It's all about parental protection. Your dad decides who would be a suitable match so you don't have to put yourself at risk."

"Then what happens?" Solana's captivated expression encouraged Hannah to continue.

"You, he, and your parents meet together in your home every week. While you get to know him better, your parents are present to chaperone. This ensures that no kissing or anything is involved."

"You can bet on that," Solana muttered under her breath.

"So you don't get to know him in private at all?" Becca took a sip of her double espresso.

"Nope. Even the letters he sends you will go through your dad first."

"Scoot," Tyler said to the girls and squeezed onto the checked vinyl couch between Solana and Becca.

"What if the guy ends up being some whacked-out weirdo?" Becca asked. When she had something to say, she just said it—no holds barred. "We had this guy at my church who my grandparents thought was perfect. He seemed nice, really helpful with the old people at church and stuff, but I always got these strange vibes from him. Then about a month ago, they found out he was stealing money from the bank accounts of all the old people who trusted him so much. What if you marry someone like that because your parents don't see who he really is and you don't find out until too late? A man like that could mess you up in a big way."

"It's not an arranged marriage, Becca," said Hannah. "You still have a choice in the matter. If you're courting you have less of a chance of mistaking a man's character because you have three viewpoints instead of one. So even if you're enamored with a guy and seeing him through rose-colored glasses, your parents might be the ones to point out the potential problems with him."

"I can't imagine that you would get a genuine look at the real person in that kind of setting." Becca had made up her mind and she wasn't going to change it. "It would be too easy to fake people out."

Solana joined in. "Isn't it weird that you only get to know him in that one setting? How do you know what he's like with his friends—or your friends? Or if he's a slob? Or how he'll treat you when the two of you are alone? I can*not* imagine not having my first private conversation with my husband until after I was married. That's crazy! You might end up getting married to some mass murderer with a skull tattooed where he sits."

Hannah sighed. She knew it would be easier to convince a mountain lion to become a vegetarian than to convince Solana on this issue.

"What's wrong with a tattoo where he sits?" asked Tyler, with a gleam in his eye. "I like mine." He spun toward Hannah. "I'm kidding," he reassured her.

She looked directly into his eyes. "What *do* you think, Tyler?"

Tyler looked back, mischief in his eyes. "About tattoos or mass murderers?"

"About *courtship*." Hannah held her breath. She hoped he was beginning to see things differently. *He's a solid Christian guy. Surely he's been listening to God's truth.*

Solana rolled her eyes.

Tyler turned away, mumbling, "I agree with Becca and Solana."

"What?" Hannah stared at Tyler in absolute disbelief. "Are you *still* going to date?"

"Why wouldn't I?"

Becca and Solana laughed. Jacie looked at her with compassion.

Hannah gripped her juice. "I thought you were reconsidering courtship after that whole mess with Jessica."

"What mess with Jessica? When did I say that?"

"Well, you said that if you would have known her better with your head before you got your heart involved, you would have saved yourself a lot of pain."

"Yeah, I said that. But I didn't mean I was going to start doing courtship. It just made me reevaluate my . . . selection process."

"Your *selection* process?" asked Hannah, astounded. "Sounds like you're picking out a new car or what you're going to have for lunch."

"It's not like that—"

"Then what is it? Why don't you change from dating to courtship? You've been hurt. That should be enough to show you what's best."

Tyler shifted uncomfortably on the sofa. A piece of blond, sun-streaked hair fell in front of his face, but he didn't bother to brush it away. He looked up with apologetic sky-blue eyes and took a deep breath. "I agree with your convictions," he began, cautiously choosing each word. "I admire how careful you are about relationships. But I haven't changed my mind. I still don't think courtship is right for everyone. And," he took another deep breath, "I *know* it's not right for me."

Hannah clenched her teeth, holding back what she really wanted to say. Becca looked at her, expectant. Solana looked smug.

Jacie leaned forward. "Not everyone has to think like you do," she said to Hannah. "It doesn't make you wrong."

Becca nodded. "Like Tyler said, we admire your choice. It's just not right for us."

Becca's comment ignited the fire within Hannah. "Oh, so now we believe in 'do whatever feels right for you'? We all believe whatever we want and that's fine? Then what makes us any different than the world? I suppose if Tyler decides that drinking is what's best for him, we should all support him?"

She knew her arguments were becoming ridiculous, but she couldn't stop herself. "As I understand it, Christians are supposed to live lives as pure and holy as we possibly can." Her voice raised an octave. "Don't you, as a Christian, agree with that?" She had been talking to Becca, but she turned and addressed the question to Tyler.

This time it was Tyler's turn to get upset. But when Tyler got upset, he didn't fly off the handle. He left the scene. "Sure, Hannah. Sure. See you guys later," he said as he stood up and sauntered out the door.

"Hey, Ty," Jacie called to Tyler's retreating back.

He turned around.

"Alyeria," she said and smiled at him.

"Alyeria," echoed Solana and Becca in unison.

Tyler looked relieved. He shot an appreciative glance at Jacie. "Alyeria," he said. He gave a quick wave and was out the door.

"He'll be okay," noted Becca. The other two nodded.

Hannah stared down at her blue-and-white checked skirt, tracing some invisible design with her finger. Whenever the four friends mentioned Alyeria, it reminded her that the she was the fifth wheel in the group. The first day of school Jacie got the attention of her friends by shouting "Alyeria" across the quad. At that moment, Hannah knew these friends were different. She later learned they were bound together by love and a grove of aspen trees at the elementary school where the four of them had met each other and created an imaginary world named Alyeria.

Jacie had once said that the group probably would have grown apart if it hadn't been for Tyler. He insisted on being loyal to each other and to a pact they'd made—even during the turbulent junior high years. He would make the girls meet at the grove to talk things out—like when

Becca developed a crush on a guy Jacie liked, or when Solana got sick of everyone trying to "shove morality down her throat."

The friendship the four of them had was more like watching three sisters interacting with their brother. He watched over them like a brother. And they teased him like one.

Hannah supposed that was why she had been so drawn to the group in the first place. Her parents had always emphasized that boys and girls her age should treat each other like brothers and sisters in Christ. It had been a nice concept, but Hannah had never seen it in action until she met this group. Now she realized that there was something different about when a guy friend—*a brother in Christ*, she corrected herself—empathizes with or encourages you, than when a sister in Christ does.

She had never been to Alyeria. Tyler had once talked about taking her, but she remembered the other girls shooting looks that could kill when he suggested it. Solana changed the subject, and Tyler never mentioned it again.

As the girls finished their drinks, Hannah knew she would never truly belong.

● ● ●

That night, Hannah moved her comfy wicker chair in her small attic bedroom close to the window. The attic was her favorite place in the world. She loved the steep stairway that led up there and the dim, almost eerie lighting. She even loved the musty smell that emanated from the old boxes and unused furniture. It was *her* place. Her preferred place to *think*.

Hannah leaned against the cold pane. The promised blizzard had weakened to a heavy snowstorm. Fat flakes floated past. If it had been summer, she would have crawled out onto the rooftop outside to look at the stars.

Why did it bother me so much what Tyler said today?

Even though the girls disagreed with her, it didn't hurt as much as when Tyler said, "I know it's not right for me." That cut deep.

Why? Is it because I secretly hope he'd like to court me someday?

Maybe because she had come to respect him so much. And now, she felt herself losing that respect.

Well, she thought as she picked up her journal. *At least I get the chance to talk about courtship in class.*

Putting aside her disappointment with Tyler and the confusing feelings that went along with it, she tried to focus on the positive aspects of the opportunity presented to her.

I believe this chance to share in my class is from God because He wants others to know about courtship—because He wants to protect every teenager from getting hurt in relationships that aren't godly. And I'm not backing down from that truth. Even if no one else agrees with me.

Tyler's face flashed before her.

Even if it is an incredibly lonely place.

chapter 4

"Rebekah, come back here. You have toothpaste in your hair." Hannah grabbed a washcloth from the sink and chased after her nine-year-old sister. She stepped over her little brother Daniel, whose race-track blocked her pursuit.

"Don't build that in the middle of the hallway, Daniel," Hannah said. "And get out of your pj's. It's almost time to leave." Daniel didn't understand why he couldn't wear pajamas to his homeschool playgroup. As a first-grader, it seemed logical to wear them all day, so when it was time for bed, he wouldn't have to change again.

Mrs. Connor headed toward the stairs, carrying four-year-old Sarah Ruth on her hip. "Hannah, would you make sure Rebekah changes her shoes? I can't believe it snowed three inches last night and she still wants to wear sandals."

Elijah, with his ever-present blankie in tow, trotted behind his mother and twin sister. He looked up at Hannah with a sleepy gaze. She leaned down and gave him a quick kiss on top of his tousled head.

"Hannah, will you French-braid my hair?" Rebekah called from her room.

"Sure, sweetie." Hannah stepped inside Rebekah's room. "But only if you change into your tennis shoes and get downstairs in two minutes." Rebekah always needed incentives to get her moving in the right direction. A colored-pencil set could distract her, and hours floated by unnoticed. Rebekah's artwork covering her shell-pink walls was proof enough of that.

Hannah held up the washcloth. "First let's get that toothpaste out of your hair." Rebekah bounced over to Hannah and stood on one foot and then the other while Hannah gently wiped the blue gel from Rebekah's hair. "I'll get the comb and meet you downstairs." She gave Rebekah an affectionate tap on the end of her nose.

"Okay," Rebekah said. "Can we use these hair bands I decorated?" She held up colorful beribboned bands.

Hannah smiled, looking into the wide cornflower-blue eyes that mirrored her own. "They're perfect," she said. She wrapped her arm around her sister's shoulder and kissed the top of her head. "But you'll need to hurry or we won't have time to use them."

Hannah trotted downstairs. She took a deep breath. Mornings in the Connor household were always like this—hectic.

Even though Mom has her hands full with six kids, I'm glad she insists we all sit down to eat breakfast. Now, if we could only eat together, *that would be the best way to start the day.*

She almost laughed. There was no way her 14-year-old brother Micah would cooperate with that.

By the time Hannah got downstairs, her lunch bag was ready and waiting next to Micah's on the blue-tiled countertop. The twins sat at the table, finishing their breakfast. A tiny bit of waffle and syrup stuck to Sarah Ruth's cheek.

"I made some of that chicken salad you like," Mrs. Connor said to

Hannah as she took a wet cloth and made the syrup disappear. Sarah Ruth pulled away from the dampness. She hated her face to be wiped.

"Thanks, Mom," Hannah said, sitting at the table. She forked a waffle onto her plate and put a piece of bacon next to it. She bowed her head and said a quick, silent prayer.

When she opened her eyes, her mother was wiping up some spilled orange juice from under Sarah Ruth's booster seat. Hannah had always admired her mother. Even during the times that would be frazzling for most mothers of six kids, Gretchen Connor always seemed under control. Today she had clipped her shoulder-length blonde hair into a barrette. Hannah noted that even this early in the morning her mom looked fresh and young.

Hannah took three bites of waffle before she smelled her brother's cologne.

"Waffles again?" he asked as he entered the busy kitchen. He wrinkled his nose. "I need to start having eggs and stuff to get in shape for wrestling. You guys and your waffles are going to bump me up into the next weight bracket." Micah pulled out a chair from the table and turned it around so he could sit down while resting his chin on the back of it.

"First of all, I don't see any 'guys' here making breakfast," Mrs. Connor replied curtly. "Secondly, if you want eggs to eat, you know where to find them."

Micah gave his irresistible half-smile, one side of his mouth curled up revealing his right dimple. "I know. But my cooking just doesn't compare to my lovely mom's and wonderful sister's."

"So you think some buttering up will get you what you want, hmm?" Hannah chimed in as she opened the refrigerator and removed a carton of eggs.

Micah was only two years younger, but she never let him forget he would always be her little brother—age-wise at least. At the moment they were the same height, but Micah had started another growth spurt and would be surpassing her any day now.

She and Micah were the only ones who left the house for school. Hannah had loved being homeschooled, but Micah had only tolerated it. Homeschooling had enabled Hannah to work at her own pace. She was quick, and usually completed all her daily assignments by noon. This left her the whole afternoon to help her younger siblings, practice her photography, or go running. But now, attending Stony Brook High School took up most of her day.

Micah, on the other hand, preferred meeting people to being stuck with his family day after day. Hannah couldn't understand this at all. Her family was very close and they were her favorite people to spend time with. Micah's boredom and social makeup often caused disturbances during homeschool. So when the Connors decided Hannah needed to attend public school to learn advanced science and math, they allowed Micah to go as well.

Hannah scrambled the eggs, adding onion and cheese the way Micah liked them. As she cooked, she thought how she admired her younger brother's coordination. He never went through the awkward stage most preteen guys did—when they're just a mess of long arms, gangly legs, and I-have-no-idea-what-to-do-with-this kind of hair. He had a dark complexion like his father's, which made the Connor signature blue eyes more prominent. His good looks drew the attention of many girls from school. Much to her parents' chagrin, these girls called Micah almost every night. Mom and Dad didn't even try to hide their disapproval. Not only was it "completely inappropriate" for young women to initiate contact with young men, but it also went against their beliefs about courtship that they had tried to instill in their children.

"What's your hurry?" Micah asked as she flipped the eggs with lightning speed from the pan to the plate and the plate to the table. "I'm not *that* hungry."

"I want to get to school early," Hannah said. "I plan to stop by the newspaper office to see if they'd like me to be one of their photographers."

"Cool," muffled Micah through a mouthful of eggs. He was so absorbed in wolfing down his breakfast in record time that Hannah wasn't sure he had heard her.

The idea had plagued her since she saw the flyer on the bulletin board outside her classroom. She gave in, talking it over with her parents last night. Now nervous butterflies made her question the idea. She hadn't mentioned it to the Brio girls, although she had almost called Jacie to get her advice. *If I don't get the job, I don't want my failure to be front-page news. The only thing that would be worse is if they felt sorry for me*, Hannah told herself.

"Hannah," Rebekah said, running to her sister. "Will you do my hair now? Please?"

"Sure, sit here." Hannah took up the comb and ran it through the long blond hair. Putting the comb into her mouth, she parted the hair into sections with expert fingers.

The phone rang, and Mrs. Connor picked it up while pouring herself a glass of orange juice. "Hello." An expression of disapproval crossed her face.

Another girl calling for Micah, Hannah thought.

"I'm sorry," her mom said. "He doesn't have time to talk right now. He's eating breakfast. Can this wait until you see him at school?"

Micah glanced at his mother while continuing to eat. Hannah couldn't read his face.

Mrs. Connor hung up the phone. She looked at Micah. "First of all, I don't enjoy people calling this early in the morning 'just to chat.' If you could discourage your friends from doing so, Micah, I would appreciate it."

Micah stared at his empty plate. Hannah could tell he knew what was coming next.

"Secondly, your father and I have told you numerous times that we do not approve of girls calling for you. If this continues, Micah, we'll tell them ourselves when we answer the phone. But it would be much easier if you would explain our wishes to them."

Micah continued staring at his plate. "I don't see what the big deal is. I have a lot of friends at school. So what if they're girls."

Hannah swallowed back a gasp. Micah was the most free-spirited of the Connor children, but this back talk stepped way over the line of acceptable behavior even for him.

"You'll do it because we said so and obedience is honoring to your father and I."

Hannah thought her mom was being generous. If her dad hadn't already left for work at the architecture firm, he would have taken Micah into the den for a "talking to."

Micah turned around. Everyone in the kitchen seemed to be holding their breath, waiting to see what he would do. Even the twins appeared to know this was serious. "Yes, ma'am," he said quietly.

"Thank you," she said. And then it was back to business. "You should get going, Hannah. Since you need to stop by the newspaper office, you can take the car today. Micah will bike to school at the normal time." She handed Hannah her lunch and gave her a quick peck on the cheek.

"Mom, what if they hate my pictures?"

Mrs. Connor put her hands on each side of Hannah's face and looked at her with affection. "Hannah. You are so hard on yourself. Relax. Let God work as He will in your life. You don't need to strive so hard."

"But I want to please Him, Mom."

"You do, sweetie. You're so talented. If this is God's will, you'll get the job. I know you'd be the best photographer that school has ever known. You know I'll be praying for you."

"Thanks, Mom." Hannah smiled. The encouragement was nice to hear, but she didn't quite believe it.

● ● ●

Hannah's steps echoed in the empty hallway as she neared the newspaper office. She still didn't know why she was doing this. She wasn't an experienced photographer, but she thought she might be good at it. *If they just give me the chance*. She clung tightly to the manila envelope that held her finest photographs—a mixture of both black-and-whites and full-colors. It had been a painstaking process to go through them all and decide which ones she liked best. Her favorites were those which captured the emotions of her younger siblings. Micah posing with his bat, determined to hit a home run; Rebekah intense as she drew with her colored pencils; Daniel playing his violin; Elijah sleepily drinking a glass of milk; Sarah Ruth with an awestruck expression while watching fireworks.

Sarah Ruth was the most difficult to photograph. If she knew Hannah had her camera out, she would walk around with a smile plastered on her face, like the Cheshire cat's, trying to get Hannah to use her as a subject.

Hannah had tried to include some variety in her portfolio—a few action shots of Tyler playing basketball at the park with the girls, some close-ups of a patch of columbines she'd discovered this past summer on one of her runs.

She ran her slender fingers along the side of the envelope as she stood in the open doorway, observing the scene before her. She recognized two kids from her English class who sat huddled in the corner, arguing about what to cut from an editorial on the dangers of intramural sports. A girl with frizzy, red hair pulled back with a headband sat facing a computer screen, her face knit in deep concentration. Another girl sat at a neighboring computer playing solitaire. Hannah wiped her sweaty palms on her long paisley skirt and tried to decide who seemed the most approachable.

Before she could choose, the frizzy-haired girl snapped her gum loudly, threw up her hands, and exclaimed, "Done!" She spun around and noticed Hannah. "Hi! Can I help you with something?"

Her easy smile made Hannah more comfortable. "Hi. I'm . . . I . . . uh . . . saw your posting for a photographer and I wanted to . . ." She didn't quite know where to go with the sentence, so she held out the manila envelope. "Here's some of my work."

"Great! We were really, like, starting to get really worried, y'know. See, the guy who used to, like, photograph for us is leaving town. Not, like, he was super great or anything, but he was decent. So this is, like, way cool." The girl smacked her gum when she talked. The other kids glanced her direction but appeared uninterested.

The frizzy-haired girl stood up and held out her hand. "By the way, my name is Megan. Well, like, actually my real name is Mabel, but you can see, like, why I'd want to change it." She made a face. "Uh-oh. I hope that's, like, not *your* name."

Hannah shook her head, amused, as Megan popped a bubble and continued.

"Now, you'd think that most people then would, like, just go by their middle name. But my middle name is Edna, and that's even, like, worse. Mabel Edna. What were my parents thinking, you wonder? Mabel was my great-aunt who my mom, like, just adored. And Edna, believe it or not, was, like, my dad's favorite pet when he was growing up. His fish of all things! So I'm named after, like, a dead goldfish. Go figure."

Hannah nodded, unsure what to say.

"Anyway, oh yeah, your pictures. This is, like, cool. No one's come in before with, like, a portfolio." She took the envelope from Hannah's still-outstretched hand. "I would, like, hire you on the spot, but I need to show them to Brendan. He's, like, our editor-in-chief." Megan rolled her eyes. "He's, like, *majorly* picky. Which is a good thing, I suppose—being in the journalism field and all. It just gets, like, annoying. Y'know? Anyway, he has a meeting with the principal right now. They have, like, this weekly thing. He interviews him for the Principal's Corner. I know . . . like, gaggy. But, anyway, he should be back really soon. Wanna cop a squat?"

Hannah didn't know what Megan meant by that until she noticed Megan was pointing to a nearby chair. Hannah nodded and sat down.

This was a new experience. In homeschooling groups she had been involved in, she never had to "audition" for anything. Everyone made the softball team—even if they didn't want to. Everyone was in the year-end plays.

Hannah settled into the chair, rehearsing what she should say to the editor and how she should convince him that she could do the job.

I know I don't have any experience working for a school newspaper, but I love photography and even took a beginning photography class at a local college back in Michigan. In here you'll find some of the photos I've taken in the last few months. There's quite a variety. I develop them—

"Lindsey, close down the solitaire." The male voice coming from outside the doorway was clearly used to being in control. "I need to have that advice column by 9:00 this morning or I'm going to have to find myself a new Dear Gabbie."

Megan nodded in Hannah's direction. "There's someone here about the photography position."

Hannah stood to meet the editor. But her well-rehearsed speech disappeared. She stood there with her mouth open, speechless. She was face-to-face with the most amazing-looking guy she had ever seen.

chapter 5

"Brendan Curtis," he said, sticking out his hand. Tall with an athletic build, he stood a good five inches above Hannah. His features were a chiseled work of art. She could see the trace of his dimples, reminding her of her brothers. *God, You did a good job on this one. Did I just say that? Sorry, God, I know I shouldn't be thinking like this. I know You have me here for a reason—to spread Your truth—not to fall for some guy. Maybe it's the work of the devil. Maybe he wants to distract me.*

Still, she couldn't help but notice the outline of Brendan's biceps under his button-up shirt. His chestnut-brown eyes, dark around the outside with flecks of gold in the middle, drew her focus. She found herself drowning in them and had to keep tearing herself away. *Now I know how Jacie felt about Damien's eyes.*

" . . . and that's pretty much the whole staff," Brendan was saying.

Uh-oh, has he been talking this whole time? I have no idea what he said.

Hannah felt sick. Butterflies were having a party in her stomach, and her mouth was stone dry. *I'm going to faint*, she thought. She envisioned this awful picture of her dropped out of consciousness onto the camel-colored tiles, or maybe slumped over a nearby desk. She would probably be drooling or something equally disgusting.

"Hannah, are you okay?" Brendan's voice broke into her daydream.

"Huh?" said Hannah, startled.

"I asked if you had any questions."

"Oh. Um . . . no. You explained it very well." *At least I assume he did.*

"Good. Can I see your photographs now?"

Hannah handed him the envelope. "Should I let you have a chance to look at them and check back with you later?" *Finally something that sort of makes sense.*

Brendan slowly flipped through the pictures. "No, I don't think that will be necessary."

The butterflies in Hannah's stomach took kamikaze dives into her shoes. *He hates them. What was I thinking? They must look so amateur.*

Brendan continued. "If you'd like the position of photographer, it's yours. These are great." He handed the manila envelope back to Hannah.

"Really?"

"Like, cool!" Megan said. She stepped onto the top of a nearby desk. "Attention everyone," she announced. "We now, like, have an official photographer for the *Stony Brook Times.* Introducing . . . what was your name again?"

"Hannah Connor."

"HANNAH CONNOR!"

The smattering of applause drifted away to the hum of people working at their computers.

"Thanks, Megan," Brendan said, and then turned to Hannah. "I guess it's official now."

Hannah nodded. Brendan's eyes looked straight through her.

"Do you have plans for this weekend?" he asked.

The question set off bells inside Hannah. Since she had begun attending Stony Brook, several boys in her classes had inquired with a similar question, which often ended in an invitation for a date. She thought of it as an opportunity to explain her beliefs in courtship, which also provided an easy way to decline their invitations. It had always been a convenient excuse before, but now she almost wished she didn't have to give it. Almost. She shook her head.

"Good," Brendan said. "We'll need you to take pictures on the ski trip."

"The ski trip?"

I'm an idiot.

"Yeah. To Breckenridge. You must have heard about it. It's this weekend."

"*This* weekend?"

"Yeah. We're leaving after school on Friday and then coming back Sunday night."

"Sunday night?"

What about church?

"Do you realize you're repeating everything I say?"

"Everything you . . . oh, sorry." Hannah could feel the hot redness coming up her neck and coloring her face.

"That's okay." Brendan seemed amused. "Since you're on staff, we can cover your cost. But we'll need a permission slip signed by your parents." He handed her the form off a nearby desk. "You can turn it in to Mrs. Platte in the office."

Brendan's confidence both relaxed and unnerved her. It was obvious he was used to getting what he wanted. He didn't ask if she wanted to come on the trip—he expected her to go. Even as they discussed film types and what camera she would bring, she felt like her comments sounded amateurish compared to his self-assured demeanor.

"If you need anything, let me know," he called as she floated out of the newspaper office toward her first class.

This weekend. But would her parents let her go off with a bunch of teenagers to stay in a hotel for a weekend?

She'd never done anything like that before. She'd never wanted to. She didn't understand the deep desire creeping into her. She wanted to go more than she'd wanted to do anything in a long time.

Mom and Dad have to let me go . . . they just have to.

• • •

"Guess what?" Hannah was glad to find her friends all together at their usual cafeteria table. She plopped her lunch down amid the milk cartons and taco salads.

"Victoria's Secret has a new line of knee-length underwear?" asked Solana.

"I got the job as the school newspaper photographer!" she said, ignoring Solana's sarcasm. A month ago, a comment like that from Solana would have cut Hannah deeply. By now she'd grown accustomed to Solana's sense of humor—and more able to accept that she was often the brunt of it.

The group reacted with enthusiasm. Even Solana seemed impressed.

"Congratulations! You didn't even tell us you were thinking about applying," Jacie said.

"I was kind of embarrassed—and afraid I wouldn't get it," admitted Hannah. "And I'm not sure about this yet, but I might go on the ski trip this weekend."

"Really?" said Tyler. "That's great!"

"I have to get my parents' permission first. So pray for me, okay? I mean, if I'm supposed to go."

The others, minus Solana, nodded.

"And pray about Thursday, too. That's when I'm giving my presentation on courtship." She settled down in her seat. "Is there anything I can be praying about for you guys?"

"I have a test in chemistry tomorrow," said Tyler, making a face.

"I think I'm coming down with a cold," added Jacie.

"I want to do my best in our game tonight," said Becca.

Hannah pulled out her prayer journal from her purse.

"I have a friend I'm kind of worried about," said Solana in a hushed voice.

Hannah looked at Solana. Usually Solana sneered when Hannah asked for prayer requests. *Maybe her heart is finally softening*, she thought.

"What are you concerned about, Solana?" she asked, leaning toward her.

"Well, my friend doesn't believe in dating, and I'm worried that she's going to end up with some mass-murderer who has a tattoo where he sits," she answered with only a hint of a smile.

Hannah shook her head as she noted in her prayer journal:

Tyler—chemistry test

Jacie—health

Becca—game

Solana—SALVATION!!!

• • •

"Hi, Mom," Hannah called as she walked in the warm house, closing the door to the blustery cold outside.

"Welcome home, sweetie," her mother called from the kitchen. Hannah smelled roast beef cooking. "Listen to the answering machine. Aunt Dinah left a message for you."

"Oh, goody!"

Aunt Dinah was her father's youngest sister. Dinah had been a "surprise" to Grandpa and Grandma, born 10 years after her closest sibling. She was, as Mr. and Mrs. Connor said, "her own person." In her late 20's, she had no plans to settle down. She worked as a public relations representative for an international company, traveling the world as part of her job. In between those trips, she would go on her own personal adventures, hardly spending any time in her small New York apartment.

It wasn't uncommon for Hannah to come home from school and find a postcard from Egypt, a package of chocolates from Italy, or a recording on the answering machine to "just say hi" from Tibet.

Dinah had sent her last postcard to Hannah from Jamaica. The front showed a group of tanned, shirtless men carrying surfboards, and the caption read, "Wish you were here!" Aunt Dinah had written on the back " . . . but I bet your dad is glad you're not!" Dinah had only sent it because she got a kick out of knowing she made her conservative older brother bristle. And bristle he did. The card ended up in the trash, where Hannah would never have seen it if she hadn't had garbage duty that night.

Aunt Dinah started out like the rest of the Connor family. She'd been raised in the same conservative home. She accepted Christ at a young age. But things changed when, as a teenager, she started getting into trouble.

A couple years ago, Aunt Dinah had come back to God. But even that hadn't affected her free spirit. If anything, it seemed to heighten it.

Hannah loved talking to Dinah about God because faith seemed more real to Aunt Dinah. She rarely quoted verses, but her conversations often sparkled with exciting experiences of God's involvement in her life. Hannah's parents said the black sheep of the family had become the orange sheep. She wasn't a "bad girl" anymore, but she sure didn't fit in with the rest of the flock.

"Hellooo, Connors!" the singsongy voice played out of the answering machine. "Or should I say *hola!* I'm calling from Costa Rica to leave a message for my sweet little Hannah. I've been wondering how school is going. It must be quite an adjustment. I wanted to let you know you've been on my heart and I've been praying for you. Oh . . . hold on a second." Hannah heard Aunt Dinah's muffled Spanish as she spoke with someone on the other end. "Okay," she said, coming back on the line. "I need to get going. My moped is about to get towed. But I love you all and I'll talk to you soon. *Hasta luego!*"

Hannah listened to the message one more time before deleting it. She loved her aunt's spunk. No one else could get away with it. Hannah couldn't imagine being so carefree.

"She's a sweetheart, isn't she?" her mom said, entering the room and wiping her hands on a dish towel.

"Yeah, she is." Hannah wouldn't have minded a little chat with her aunt right now. Maybe she could tell Aunt Dinah about Brendan. Maybe.

"So how was your day?" Mom asked.

"Well, there's something I want to talk to you about."

● ● ●

"What do you think?" Hannah glanced from her dad to her mom and then back to her dad. It was after dinner and the three were seated in her father's den, where all serious conversations took place. Mr. Connor looked at the wall behind Hannah, a slight frown on his face as he processed her request.

"I don't know, Hannah. Allowing my daughter to spend a weekend with a group of non-Christians whom I don't know doesn't seem wise."

Hannah's heart sank. In the Connor home, Mr. Connor's word was law. Hannah didn't want to argue with him. She respected her father's views on things, but she also thought he was being too protective in this situation. *He hasn't actually said the word "no" yet*, she reminded herself.

"You know Jacie and Becca," she said, intentionally leaving out Solana's name. "And some kids from our church youth group are going. It's going to be well-chaperoned by adults. I can get you their phone numbers if you want."

Her dad looked toward her. Hannah couldn't read his expression. She took his silence as an opportunity to continue.

"Dad, I'll respect whatever decision you make. I know you have my best interests in mind. But please remember that this is my first chance to use my photography skills." Hannah could feel the emotion coming into her voice, and she finished with a thought she knew her dad would approve of. "And being on the newspaper staff will allow me to influence the entire school for Christ." She looked at her mother. "Mom? You were on the newspaper staff at your school."

Her mother shook her head. "Which is precisely why I'm concerned, as well. I know better than anyone what can happen on these trips." She bit her lip. "The world is full of dangers, sweetie. As your parents we need to protect you from as many of them as possible."

Hannah dropped her head. "I know. But I really think I can handle this now. I think I'm a strong enough Christian to stand up to whatever could happen." She looked up, first at her mom, then her dad. "You've raised me well. My faith is solid."

"Let me talk it over with your mother and think about it some more," Mr. Connor said. He smiled and reached over to ruffle her hair.

Hannah tried to return a smile at her father's affectionate dismissal. "I'll be upstairs doing my homework. Thank you for listening." She left the room not knowing which way it would go. She'd given it her best argument.

Hannah read a chapter out of her Bible, like she did every evening, and then picked up her journal.

I never doubted Mom and Dad before. I've always had complete trust in their authority and decisions. And I still do . . . I think. I wonder if they understand how important this trip is to me. I want to fit in at Stony Brook. I don't want to be like the other kids, but I do want to feel like I'm a part of the school somehow. And I love the idea of taking pictures that are for something important—not to be stuffed in photo albums and looked at once a year. I still trust Mom and Dad. I still believe they want the best for me. I'm just not sure that I believe they know what that is.

chapter 6

Hannah stood in front of Mrs. Platte's desk, waiting for her weekend room assignment. She shifted her weight from one foot to the other. She still couldn't believe her parents had said yes. "We've decided to let you know we trust you completely," her father had said before leaving for work that morning. Hannah had thrown her arms around his neck. He returned the hug and kissed her cheek. "Take good pictures and make us proud."

Hannah leaned on Mrs. Platte's desk. "Are you sure there's room?" she asked as the secretary scanned the computer screen.

"Oh yes, Hannah. Brendan told me to leave a space open for you. You're the last person to sign up . . . Let me see who has an available room." Her plump finger tapped the screen. "Here's one. Do you know Solana Luz?"

Solana Luz?

Oh great. Just what I wanted. To room with someone who will make snide remarks about me all weekend.

"Yes I do, Mrs. Platte. That will be fine."

She took the printout from Mrs. Platte and folded it. She left the office, tucking the paper into her purse, next to her prayer journal.

She'd been praying about Solana's salvation for months now. Maybe rooming with Solana was the answer to her prayer. Maybe Solana would see how Hannah lived out her faith and have questions for her. Maybe this was all part of God's plan. She remembered one of her father's favorite sayings: "I don't believe in coincidence, but I do believe in the hand of God."

● ● ●

"Don't expect me to pray with you every night," Solana said, shooting a hard look toward Hannah. The Brio friends grouped around their lunch table.

"Of course not. But if you ever want to, let me know," Hannah replied.

"Oh, brother," Solana muttered. "This is going to be a long weekend."

"This is great!" Jacie said, flashing her famous grin. "With you two sharing a room, it'll be easier for all of us to hang out." She and Becca had signed up to room together.

"Yeah. We can still have our regular Friday night hangout time," Becca said. The group's Friday evening tradition was to go to Becca's and have pizza, talk, play air hockey, and watch movies on the McKinnons' big screen television.

"And I can help you with your skiing," volunteered Tyler.

Hannah noticed Solana making a face at Becca.

"Thanks, Tyler," Hannah replied.

Between taking pictures, working with Brendan, rooming with

Solana, and skiing with Tyler, this was going to be an interesting weekend.

• • •

That evening, Hannah wrote notes for her courtship presentation the next day. It was pretty easy. She jotted down quotes from a number of books on the subject and things her parents had told her for years. If there was anything she could speak knowledgeably about, this was it. She put the note cards into a file folder, placed it next to her backpack where she wouldn't miss it, and settled into her big wicker chair.

She closed her eyes, remembering when she became truly aware that courtship meant she would behave differently from other kids. She and her friends were probably in the seventh grade, hanging out at a company picnic. Their parents were nearby, squeezed around a picnic table overflowing with barbecued chicken and potato salad when one of the young teen girls walked by holding hands with a boy.

Sarah's parents mentioned how cute it was that their daughter was so smitten. They talked about the changes that would soon take place when she actually started dating.

Mr. Connor said that he didn't know about the other girls, but Hannah would not go the usual route of dating. Sarah's parents looked at each other.

"Why not?" Mr. Washington asked.

Mr. Connor explained that dating encouraged girls to give their hearts too early, too freely, and without restraint. "We want our daughter to be constantly aware that there is only one man she will give her heart to."

Deborah's and Aubrey's parents readily agreed, while Sarah's, and the other parents wholeheartedly disagreed. A rousing discussion followed as the girls tried to listen without their parents knowing.

In the end, Sarah walked around the lake holding hands with the boy while Hannah watched as if viewing life on another planet. She agreed with her parents; that life was not for her.

Hannah thought about that day and how it had changed her life. From then on, she looked at boys differently—as though they were on the other side of a wall she dare not scale. Not yet.

● ● ●

Hannah smoothed her skirt as Ms. Bennett took roll, then returned and discussed yesterday's homework assignment. *Lord, please help me to speak truth in a way that will convict my fellow students and encourage them to see You as more significant in their relationships, even if I can't say Your name.* It sounded a lot like her father's prayer from the night before during family devotions. Her parents had been excited about this opportunity. She didn't want to disappoint them—or God.

"Today we're going to do something a little different. Hannah Connor," Ms. Bennett stretched out her hand in Hannah's direction, "will be sharing with us her views on courtship. Hannah?"

Hannah picked up her folder of notes and headed toward the front of the room while Ms. Bennett continued. "Now, I don't think I need to remind you that whether you agree or disagree with Hannah's viewpoint, we should all listen with respect."

Hannah didn't realize until she got to the front that she had no place for her notes. She couldn't have them open in front of her without a podium of some sort, but she hadn't even thought about the fact Ms. Bennett never used one. She lay the folder on the teacher's desk and leaned against the front of it.

A boy by the door raised his hand. "Is this how they dated in the Dark Ages?"

"I'll be more than happy to answer your questions at the end of my presentation." Hannah surprised herself with the confidence and force that resonated from her voice. She was glad that the desk was behind her to steady her. She felt like her whole body was shaking. *Here it goes.*

"Many of you are probably unfamiliar with the term courtship and what it means. Or perhaps you believe it is old-fashioned and not applicable to the way dating is done today. I hope by the end of this class period you'll see what I have come to believe—courtship is not only normal, but also the healthiest way to meet your future mate."

The rest of the class passed in a blur. Hannah soon realized she didn't need her notes. She had heard about and discussed courtship so much, it was very natural to talk about its benefits. She spoke with ease about the dangers of dating, and how courtship remedied many of the pitfalls of physically-based relationships.

Hannah could have gone on for two hours, but Ms. Bennett interrupted her after 20 minutes. "Hannah, we only have five minutes left of class. Perhaps you should open it up for questions now."

A number of hands went up around the class. Many of them belonged to students that Hannah would rather not address.

Amber, a thin girl with straight black hair, sat in the second row, her long arm raised gracefully toward the ceiling. Hannah remembered Amber as one of the more vocal members on the student council. On the first day of class she had asked if they would be talking about homosexuality. Yesterday she had circulated a petition requesting that condoms be distributed at school. Hannah decided she would call on everyone else and hoped the bell rang before Amber had a chance to speak. Hannah nodded toward an overweight girl with freshly-permed hair instead.

"I don't get how you say courtship is so much better." The girl looked around as if flustered that everyone was staring at her. But she took encouragement from those who nodded in agreement. "I mean, it seems like the more people you date, the more you'll find out what kind of person you want to marry."

"Think of dating like a piece of Scotch tape," Hannah said, remembering an illustration her parents had used to explain it to her when she was younger. "The more people you date, the more people you stick to.

Then, after a while, your tape loses its stickiness. And you can't stick to anyone anymore."

"I'm not following," Amber spoke up, lowering her hand. "What does dating have to do with Scotch tape?" Her eyes narrowed as she spoke, and Hannah knew she was engaging in a battle.

"When you date, you connect with a lot of people. Even if it's not physical, but only an emotional connection, you give yourself away to people you aren't going to marry. And then you have little or nothing to give to the one you are going to spend the rest of your life with. You don't stick. Dating trains you for divorce, not for a lifelong marriage."

A teddy bear-type football player piped up. "I pretty much agree with the physical part. But I don't see how you can lose that part of yourself, emotionally I mean."

"Yeah," volunteered a girl named Kacey. "Like when I get upset about something, I have friends I talk to—both guys and girls. That's not wrong."

"Casual friendships are acceptable," explained Hannah, noticing Amber's cocky smile. "But there's a fine line between that and sharing your heart with a boy. Because when he comforts you after you share those kinds of things with him, it builds a connection between the two of you. And that connection could develop into a romantic interest."

"But why would that be a bad thing?" Kacey asked.

"Because neither of you is in a place where you're ready to get married. So you wouldn't enter a relationship with that intention. And if marriage isn't your intention, you shouldn't pursue romantic entanglements."

Kacey's friend Alyssa piped up. "So you mean we shouldn't even get to know a guy unless we think we might marry him?"

"Correct. But there's more to it than that. He must also have a relationship with your family and adhere to the same beliefs. He then obtains approval to court you from your parents. He'll go to your dad and talk to him about getting to know you better with the intention of committing his life to you," Hannah explained.

"Yikes, I'm only 14!" a boy in the back exclaimed amid a number of similar reactions.

"And I hate talking to dads," added another.

"Since your parents know you better than anyone, they would have the best idea if someone would be good for you," insisted Hannah. She realized she was going to lose the no-dating battle, so she decided to try for the parental involvement aspect.

Kacey raised her hand and Hannah motioned in her direction.

"My parents have the perfect guy picked out for me. He's about four inches shorter than me and has hair like my Uncle Elbert," she said.

"But what about his character? What kind of person is he?"

"He's polite enough around my parents, but when they're not around, his favorite thing to do is show me how many woodwind instrument noises he can make with just his armpit and a straw."

The class groaned, including some boys who probably did the same thing.

"Can I say something?" asked Amber, her voice sharp. She continued without waiting for a response. "I think you're giving teenagers bad advice. Here we are, trying to be independent from our parents—working hard to have freedom—and you're dragging us right back under their complete control."

Hannah noticed with concern the bobbing heads of captivated students.

Amber stood up and assumed her political tone of voice. "You're trying to erase all the independence we've worked hard to earn just so we can go tell Mommy and Daddy, 'Please pick me out a boyfriend. I can't do it myself.' I'll tell you this, it's been me—not my parents—who have picked out my friends since I was four. And I don't plan on stopping now."

Several students applauded. Hannah felt like someone had slugged her in the stomach. She struggled to respond. "Like I said, this isn't for right now. It's for when we're at an age where marriage is possible—"

"Which means we'll be even more mature and ready to handle our decisions." Amber sat down, a triumphant smirk on her face.

It was as if Amber had set the entire room on fire. Comments popped up all over the class.

"How do you know what kind of man you want for a husband if you don't date around and figure out what works best with your personality?"

"We're teenagers! What's wrong with just going out and having fun?"

"Why should we trust our parents so much? They can be deceived, too."

"You're taking life way too seriously—loosen up!"

One voice broke through clearer than the rest, silencing all the others. "If you don't believe in dating, why do I always see you hanging out with Tyler Jennings?"

chapter 7

Hannah felt her face transform into the color of a beet. *Why doesn't the bell ring?* "Tyler and I . . . we're not dating." She tried to throw in an amused laugh, but it sounded more like she was choking. "He's my brother in . . ." Hannah paused, remembering she couldn't say Christ. "He's like a brother."

"What an excuse!" someone shouted.

"Girlfriend, do you have another brother that hot that you'd like to share with the rest of us?" one girl piped up.

Comments and questions came at her too fast. Before Hannah could regain control of the discussion, the bell rang. Hannah watched Amber collect her books and walk out of the room with her head held high, tossing her hair over her shoulder as she giggled with a friend.

God, I don't know why I did this, but I'll just trust that You wanted me to, Hannah prayed silently. As she gathered her things she felt someone beside her. She turned to see a petite girl with green eyes and short blonde-highlighted hair. Hannah recognized her as one of the popular girls in the class, but also knew her to be on the quieter side. Hannah remembered her name was Kelli.

Here it comes, God. Another critical comment. Another jab. Hannah's body tightened.

"Hannah." Kelli's softness took Hannah off guard. "I wanted to say thanks." She must have noticed Hannah's surprised look, because she continued quickly. "I mean, I know I didn't stick up for you earlier, but I wanted you to know that I agree with a lot of what you're saying." She paused, and Hannah saw deep emotion cross her face.

"I was . . . I am . . . one of those girls you were talking about. And there are a lot of things I regret." A single tear made its way down Kelli's freckled nose, which she wiped away. Hannah put her hand on Kelli's arm and nodded empathically. Kelli's voice choked. "I'm a Christian, and I want to live that way, but . . ." Her words trailed off.

The next class was trickling in. "I should get going," Kelli said, as though aware of how vulnerable she had become.

"Kelli," Hannah began. She didn't want the girl to leave with so many things unresolved. She didn't want Kelli to step back into the busy hallway and return to doing things she hated because she didn't know how to become something better. "Why don't you give me a call sometime? We can talk about this more if you want to."

Kelli looked up at her, her childlike eyes nearly breaking Hannah's heart.

"Really?"

Hannah nodded.

"I'd like that. Thanks." Kelli looked relieved.

Hannah jotted down her phone number on a half piece of notebook paper. "I'll be expecting to hear from you."

● ● ●

Hannah decided her presentation wasn't a total failure. The conversation with Kelli was encouraging, but she could still see the looks some of the students had given her—like Amber. Looks that told her they thought she was only a strange visitor to their planet. Even now, as she looked down at her ruffled blouse and long skirt, she knew she was different. She knew she was more conservative. She knew people made fun of her. She knew they shot amused looks at each other at her expense. Sometimes it didn't matter that she was the odd one. After all, Christ had said that people who followed Him would all be persecuted. But sometimes it did matter—a lot. A lot more than she would ever share with her mom and dad, because it seemed un-Christlike to be so concerned about what other people thought. After all, Jesus didn't care what others thought, did He?

She thought about the WWJD key chain in her purse. There were times when she didn't want to have her prayer time, when she didn't want to share the Good News with the lady in front of her in the grocery store line, when she didn't want to wear the long skirt—she wanted to wear something different. *But what would Jesus do? He would have His prayer time, He would share the Good News, He would wear the long—well, maybe not. But Jesus wouldn't give up. No, Jesus would press on.*

"Hannah! Hannah Connor!"

Hannah turned around to see who called her name in the crowded hallway.

"Girl, you look like you're on a mission," said Brendan, catching up with her.

All Hannah's thoughts vanished from her mind as Brendan stood there looking at her as though they were the only two people in the world. He was close enough that she could smell his rugged, woodsy cologne—perfect for him.

"Just lost in thought." She smiled, feeling shy. She wished she was wearing something a little more cute, a little more stylish. Or even less "farm-wifey," as Solana referred to her wardrobe. She stopped herself, forming a quick, silent prayer. *How can I be so shallow? Lord, forgive me for caring about such foolish things as clothing styles.*

They started moving together down the hallway. "I wanted to let you know we're going to have a newspaper staff meeting after school today. We have one every Thursday."

"Great!"

"We'll talk some more about the ski trip, future assignments, ideas for next week's edition, stuff like that."

"Great!"

I must sound like a moron. Come on, brain. Think of something else to say.

"Well, I'm glad to see you're so happy about it. Some people don't come with the best attitudes, so maybe you'll rub off on them." He gave her shoulder a squeeze.

"Great!"

Great.

● ● ●

"So how'd it go?" Jacie asked. Her Brio friends were waiting for her at their usual spot in the quad.

Her thoughts were still on Brendan. "What?"

"Teaching class. Y'know, what you've been talking about nonstop for the past three days," said Becca.

The expectant looks switched Hannah's thoughts from Brendan to the classroom. "I survived," she said, forcing a smile. As she did, she realized she really did feel a little better. Running into Brendan had made the whole day seem brighter. "Overall, it went pretty well. It wasn't easy, but I think it was what I was supposed to do." She dropped her backpack and took a seat at the table.

The girls asked a few more questions about how people responded. Distracted by Tyler's distance and nonreaction, she gave them vague answers.

They hadn't spoken much since the afternoon at the Copperchino.

They had both apologized the following day but hadn't had a conversation since then. There was still an awkwardness between them that hurt. She didn't know what else to say. *If he wants to talk to me, he'll have to say something first*, she decided.

For all I know he could be furious with me.

She hated the strain, but she felt stuck in it.

The conversation shifted to the topic of the weekend's ski trip, and soon Hannah excused herself to go to the newspaper staff meeting. She arrived as others were beginning to trickle in.

Brendan flashed her a quick smile from the front of the room. He began the meeting and immediately had everyone's undivided attention. As he went through assignments, critiques, and comments on the last issue, and his vision for the upcoming issues, he looked so comfortable—so in control. *So different than I must have come across when I spoke in health class*, Hannah thought, trying to shove away the memory of the awkward moments in class earlier that day.

After Brendan dismissed everyone, Hannah lingered, hoping Brendan would come talk to her. As she gathered her things, she rehearsed other words besides "great." *Wonderful. Fantastic. Super . . . no, not super.*

"Yeah, one of my friends was in that class, too," a male voice said behind her. "That chick must be really whacked out."

"The sad thing is, I hear she's pretty hot—in that wholesome kind of way," another boy said.

"I hope she doesn't turn all the girls in school to her courtship way of thinking. I couldn't handle it."

A third voice jumped in. "Don't worry about it, man. My girlfriend was in that class and she said no one took it seriously."

Hannah felt like her ears had been set on fire.

"Don't even dream, dude. This one's a regular Laura Ingalls Wilder."

"Or more like Laura Ingalls Not-very-wild-at-all."

The three guys laughed while Hannah sat frozen in her chair, a lump growing in her throat.

• • •

"Kelli Hendricks is on the phone for you," her mother said, peeking into the dining room where Hannah sat at the table surrounded by neat piles of homework assignments.

"Hi, Kelli!" Hannah said.

Kelli was apparently in no mood for niceties. "I talked to my parents about the courtship thing," she said sullenly.

"What did they say?" Hannah pictured enthusiastic responses and warm hugs.

"They thought it was . . . well, they thought it was weird. My dad said I would know the guys better than he would, anyway. And my mom said they would tell me if they didn't like somebody, but until then they'll trust my judgment."

This is very wrong, thought Hannah. "Did you tell him about the father being the gatekeeper—"

"Yes!" Kelli sounded exasperated. "They said boys always put up a front for the fathers. It's not like my parents don't want to be involved; they just want me to learn to make my own decisions."

She must have miscommunicated something. "Did you tell them about the tape example?" Hannah asked.

"Yes, Hannah. They thought it was stupid. They dated a lot and they have a great marriage. They said they 'stick' just fine."

"But the mistakes can hurt you so much."

"They think that I'll learn from my mistakes. 'That's how we all grow' they said. And you know what?" Kelli continued. "It kind of does make sense."

"They must not understand. It's not like that at all. Can you put them on the phone?"

"No. Listen, Hannah, thanks for all your help. You know, everyone gets burned sometimes—that's life. And someday the right guy will come along. But until then, maybe I'll just enjoy getting to know other people."

"But what about—"

"No more questions right now, Hannah, okay? I want to think through some things on my own."

● ● ●

After hanging up, Hannah collected her schoolwork and went to her room.

One courtship convert gained. One courtship convert gone. God, where did I go wrong? And why do You seem to be making this so hard? I only want to do what You asked me to do.

Kelli's father didn't want to participate? It had to be that he didn't understand all that courtship entailed and how it was his responsibility to protect his daughter. And poor Kelli didn't know enough about courtship yet to be able to tell them about it. Should she call Kelli's parents and explain it to them? No, that would be too forward. Perhaps a letter would be more appropriate.

Hannah chose a clean sheet of lavender stationery from her desk drawer and picked up her pen.

Dear Mr. Hendricks,

You have not yet been acquainted with me, but I am a friend of your daughter's and have something important to share with you . . .

chapter 8

Hannah and Jacie sat near the front of the bus. A whirlwind of kids swirled around them, chattering up a storm, laughing, and launching various objects from one end of the bus to the other. It was as though the pent-up energy from a week of school was released all at once. Excitement about a weekend of skiing supercharged everyone—everyone except Hannah. Even Jacie seemed more hyper than usual, laughing with some girls across the aisle, jabbering about the season's first trip to the slopes. It was like they were speaking an entirely different language.

"Jacie, what does 'spraying powder' mean?" Hannah asked. "Or 'catching some air'?"

Jacie explained, her hands waving about, demonstrating the angle of the skis and the jumps and the adrenaline rush it all brought about.

Hannah laughed. "Well, that makes sense."

"There's a lot to learn. How can you know the terms when you've never skied?"

"All I could think of was when my little sister Rebekah decided she wanted to catch air and keep it as a pet."

Lauren turned around in her seat and hung over the back. "Your sister did what?"

"She wanted air for a pet. So she went out in the backyard swinging a container, then quickly covered it with a paper plate. She kept her pet 'air' in a jar for a week."

"What happened then?" Jacie asked.

Hannah laughed. "I shouldn't laugh—it was so mean, but it was so funny. My brother Micah, who is a horrible tease, told her she'd killed it because there weren't any holes in the jar for the air to breathe through."

"I know Micah," Lauren said. "That's *your* brother?"

"Yes he is." Hannah wondered at the look on the girl's face. Did she like her brother?

"He is so sweet," Lauren said.

"He is?" Hannah asked. "He's a handful at home."

"Isn't that a brother's job?" Jacie asked.

Lauren nodded. "My brothers are both major pains. They are constantly trying to get in my face. When I was little they always thought it was fun to make me scream. Whether it was sticking bugs in my face or sneaking up behind me or kicking over whatever I'd made, my screams made them happier than anything else."

"Maybe I'm glad I don't have a brother," Jacie said.

"You are," Lauren assured her.

"I don't know," Hannah said. She'd never thought of life without her brother. There certainly would be fewer fights. Life would be more peaceful. But Micah made her think.

"Where is he?" Lauren asked, glancing around the bus.

"Grounded," Hannah said, embarrassed.

Lauren tipped her head back and laughed. "I like him more already."

Hannah opened her mouth to say something, then closed it. She didn't know how to respond to someone who thought rebellion attractive. But then, she didn't know how to respond to the kids at school, anyway.

She looked around the bus. Everyone except Jacie had on new ski gear. Matching hats and coats, with goggles hanging from their necks even though they wouldn't be used until tomorrow.

As if reading her mind, Lauren pointed at Hannah's new jacket. "Where'd you get yours?" she asked.

"Grand West Outfitters."

"I got mine there." She looked at Jacie. "You too?"

Jacie shook her head. "Goodwill. Last year."

Jacie had little money, but she shopped well, buying the newest, trendy clothes on sale from Raggs by Razz. But for the more expensive items like jackets and boots she ducked into Goodwill.

"Oh," Lauren said and smiled. She turned back to Hannah and pointed at her own bright fuchsia pink jacket. She rolled her eyes. "It was so *hard* to choose."

Hannah nodded. She had found it difficult to choose because she had no idea there would be so many bright colors and designs. After over an hour of fighting their way past all the bold fluorescent clothes, she and her mother finally found something a little more to Hannah's liking. She ran her hand along the vinyl, navy-blue and brick-red sleeve. She liked the two-tone jacket. It had design without being flashy. Her mother had laughed, saying Hannah would probably stand out on the slopes anyway because she was the only one wearing normal colors.

Oh well, thought Hannah. *I'm used to being the one who sticks out. Right now everyone is probably wondering, "Why's she on the bus? She's not like the rest of us."*

A balled up wad of paper hit Lauren in the head. "Hey!" she called out. She ducked from view, searching for the paper. In a flash, a war of paper wads broke out on the bus.

"Not your kind of thing, is it?" Jacie asked, slumping down into the seat to avoid a direct hit.

Hannah followed her lead. "Not really." She smoothed her hands over her pants.

"Cute pants," Jacie told her.

"Goodwill," Hannah said, smiling.

Jacie smiled back. "Why don't you wear pants more often?"

Hannah shrugged her shoulders. "I like skirts better."

Jacie's mouth dropped open. "Really?"

"They're more comfortable, feminine, and modest."

"You're right about them being feminine and modest, but I'd have to disagree about them being comfortable. Give me a good pair of jeans any day."

Hannah shook her head. "Not me. I don't even own a pair of jeans."

"Why? Is it against your rules?"

If Solana had asked the same question, it would have sounded harsh and mocking. But Jacie had this honest curiosity about things.

"No," Hannah said, hesitating. She pictured the laminated rule list on the family refrigerator, seeing it in her head. She hadn't looked at it in a long time. "But my parents do encourage us to wear skirts. They've taught us that skirts are more appropriate for a girl to wear. My dad says that if God had wanted men and women to dress alike, He would have created us with the same bodies."

"That's true," Jacie said. "But pants can be very feminine."

Hannah mulled that over in her head. "I don't know," she said. "Truth is, I still prefer wearing skirts."

"I know you wear pants sometimes, but would you rather wear skirts for *everything?*"

"No," Hannah laughed. "I'd rather wear pants when I play in the snow or run and stuff like that. But I'm always glad to get back home and put on a skirt."

"I love dresses, but I'm always glad to get home and put on my favorite jeans," Jacie told her. "I can't curl up and draw in a dress. I feel so stifled and uncreative when I'm wearing them. I am *so* much more creative when I'm in something comfortable. Dresses to feel feminine, comfy jeans to feel the inspiration."

Hannah almost asked her if she thought God approved of skirts over pants, but then decided she'd keep quiet about that. If Jacie wore pants, she obviously didn't think God cared. But He did, didn't He? After all, their family's favorite saying was about being 'in the world but not of it.' That *must* include modest, appropriate dress.

The girls across the row started talking to Jacie. Hannah closed her eyes and let the potpourri of conversations around her float through her head. She heard discussions about TV shows she'd never seen, music artists she'd never heard, gossip about people she'd never met. She'd always thought such conversations were stupid and shallow. *So why am I wanting to be a part of them? Why do I want to be accepted into this group of people I hardly know? Why in the world should it matter? I know who I am. I don't want to, don't need to change.*

She shook off the thoughts tempting her to become what she shouldn't. She faced them with the best weapon she knew and always used at times like these—prayer.

God, I want to be a light to these people. But I don't know how. Or where I should begin. Kelli's face suddenly came to her mind. She smiled at how God did stuff like that with her. *Thank You for allowing me to have conversations with Kelli about courtship. You know I'm trying to be a light to her by sharing my views. Courting is best, and she needs to know that.*

Hannah sat up higher in her seat, admiring the beauty of the snow-covered mountains. The astounding view brought her thoughts into a clearer focus. *Maybe that's all You want me to do this weekend, God. Maybe there will be someone else who will need to hear about courtship, someone else that I can protect from getting hurt again. Lord, please show me that person.*

An empty CapriSun slammed into the back of Hannah's head, interrupting her prayer. She turned around, her gaze locking with Brendan's.

She spun to face front again, her face flaming hot. *This is going to be harder than I thought.*

Jacie turned to her. "Angie and Melissa saw some of your photographs, Hannah. They thought they were really good." The girls across the aisle nodded in unison. The two best friends always seemed to be joined at the hip and had the same opinions about everything.

"Absolutely," Angie said.

"Totally," echoed Melissa.

"Jacie," a deep voice broke in above them. Hannah didn't even have to look up to know who it was. Her breath caught in her throat.

"Could I trade places with you for a second, Jacie? I need to talk to Hannah."

"Sure, Brendan," Jacie smiled. She glanced back at Hannah, as if trying to catch some telepathic permission signal.

Jacie moved back a row, and Brendan slid next to Hannah. "I wanted to apologize for hitting you in the head. Greg threw that at me, and I was trying to get him back. I guess my aim isn't that great."

Hannah didn't know where to look. She stared at the maze of creases in the seat in front of her. She knew it was rude to not look at him, but she didn't know if she could. She forced herself to turn toward him. "That's okay."

Brendan relaxed. "I'm really glad you're working with us, Hannah. I think you're going to do a great job."

Hannah looked down at her hands. She loved the way he said her name. "Thanks. I hope so."

There was a pause. Hannah didn't want him to leave. She wanted to talk to him more than anything. But why should he stay? She didn't know what else to say. *Should I say anything?*

In the world but not of it.

Maybe I shouldn't talk to him about anything but the newspaper.

Brendan caught a paper wad and cast it over the back of his head without looking to see where it went.

"I've brought color film as well as black-and-white," Hannah said suddenly. "I thought perhaps we might be able to have photos in the yearbook, too."

"Good thinking."

In the world but not of it.

Hannah swallowed. *Why, oh why do I want to keep him here? He said his apology. Why would he want to say anything else?* There were a ton more things to talk about with the other kids on the bus—like TV shows, singers, and school gossip. What did she and Brendan even have in common?

In the world but not of it. In the world but not of it, she kept repeating to herself, her emotions having a tug-of-war inside her. Then it came to her.

I'm attracted to him, aren't I?

The realization gave her a funny feeling in the pit of her stomach.

How can I be attracted to him? These feelings go against everything I believe about courtship. These feelings should be saved for my future husband. Not some guy I barely know.

Brendan's voice scattered her thoughts. "You seem like a really interesting person. But I don't know anything about you. Where did you move from, anyway?"

And so began a conversation that lasted the rest of the bus ride. They talked about Michigan, each other's families, living in Copper Ridge. They laughed about things that had happened during Spirit Week, and Brendan told her stories about huge mistakes the newspaper staff had made.

"So it actually went to print like that? With a picture of Snoopy and Charlie Brown on the front page?" Hannah laughed. "What was the caption?"

"That was the kicker," Brendan said, his whole being animated. "It said 'Principal Shaw greets the new superintendent.' "

Hannah laughed harder.

"We really meant to change it back to the real photo before they took it to the printer, but it just slipped our minds." He rolled his eyes, remembering. "We got in so much trouble."

The bus screeched to a stop before Hannah could ask what had happened next. "Are we here already?"

"Yeah. That went pretty quick." Brendan sounded surprised.

Hannah nodded.

"Well," he said, standing in the aisle. "Guess I'd better get my stuff. See you tomorrow!"

"Okay," she said, wondering if he was as reluctant to go as she was.

chapter 9

"Pizza's here!" Becca called through the closed door.

Hannah flung open the door, allowing the tempting scents of pepperoni and melted cheese to waft into the room.

"Great. I'm starved!" Hannah told Jacie and Becca as she took the box from them and set it down on the little hotel dresser.

"And you'll still keep your perfect figure," said Jacie, wrinkling her nose. She patted her own mostly flat stomach. "What I would do to look like you."

Hannah couldn't understand Jacie's struggle with self-esteem. Many times she'd tried to tell Jacie that she was special just because God created her. Jacie would respond as if she understood, but Hannah could tell it didn't impact her very much. Jacie was very cute and a lot of fun. Of all the girls in the Brio gang, she was the most well-liked by people at school—teachers and students—but she was also the one who was least aware of her own popularity. She would often say things, even in a funny way, that demonstrated how self-conscious she was about her appearance, her intelligence, even her artistic skill—which, in truth, was nothing short of amazing.

Hannah didn't identify with this at all. She had never doubted her own value. She had a higher self-esteem than most kids her age, and maybe that's why she felt free to speak up and let her opinions be known. She credited it to her upbringing. Her family had been her peer group, and they had always accepted her and given her unconditional love.

"Where's Solana?" Becca asked, taking a peek into the open door of the bathroom.

"Oh, Marcus called about ten minutes ago and asked her to dinner. And . . ."

" . . . she couldn't resist," finished Becca. "If we had a nickel for every time she dissed us for a guy, just think of what we could do."

"We could feed the entire country of Sudan," volunteered Hannah.

"Or at least get a new mountain bike," contributed Becca.

Jacie passed out napkins to the other girls. "I think we should put it toward some hormone repellant for Solana. I seriously worry about her."

"You do, too?" Hannah handed Becca a stringy slice of pizza. "I thought you believed in dating."

"We do, Hannah," said Becca, almost exasperated. "And we're not opposed to her going out. We just know Solana can go a little fast with guys."

Hannah's mouth opened and her voice lowered to a whisper. "You think Solana would actually have . . . sex?"

"She hasn't yet. And we hope she waits until she's married. But she has been less-than-innocent on some dates."

"And, unfortunately, a lot of guys know it." Jacie took a bite of her pizza.

"Um, Jacie," Hannah said. "Can we say grace first?"

"Oh, sorry," Jacie swallowed. "I forgot. Go ahead."

Hannah prayed a blessing on the food and also prayed for protection over Solana. When she finished, she looked at the other two with wide-eyed concern. "What do we do for her?"

"Just what we have been doing," said Becca. "Keep being her friend, keep being honest with her about what we think is best for her, and keep bringing up our faith whenever the opportunity arises."

"And living out our faith in front of her—showing her love and compassion," added Jacie.

"But those things alone aren't working. I mean . . . you've been friends with her for seven years now," insisted Hannah. "Isn't there something else we can do?"

"Well, we're not going to start chaperoning her," said Becca, getting a little defensive.

"I don't know," joked Jacie. "Maybe we could all get sunglasses, trench coats, and spy equipment and follow her around."

"Then if she starts making out with some guy, we'll shine our high-powered flashlight beams on her." Becca was getting into the idea now.

Now it was Hannah's turn to become a little defensive. "Seriously, you guys. She could make a huge mistake and be really hurt. Boy-girl relationship can be very damaging at our age."

"Hey, watch what you're saying," Becca said. "I happen to be dating someone, y'know."

"You and Nate are different," Hannah said.

Jacie stretched out on the bed. "So it's okay to date if you do it like Becca and Nate?"

"No, I don't think dating is okay, period. But they're different—not as horrible as how Solana dates."

Becca rolled her eyes. "You flatter me with your outpouring of compliments."

Jacie smirked. "Yeah, Becca, you're not horribly evil, just that basic kind of evil."

Becca laughed, wiping her greasy fingers on a napkin. "Speaking of evil, what's going on with you and Damien?"

"Nothing." Jacie folded her arms over her chest, not hiding the disappointment in her voice. "And I'm sticking to it. I won't even think about having a relationship with him until he becomes a stronger Christian."

"Does he like going to church with you?" asked Hannah, munching on her crust. Despite Damien's rough exterior, she appreciated that he was always real with her.

"Yeah, he likes both church and The Edge," Jacie said, referring to the once-a-month rally with a bunch of local youth groups. "He loves hanging out there."

"So, Hannah—" Becca swallowed the bite in her mouth before posing the question. "Would you say Jacie and Damien are dating when they go to The Edge together?"

"No, because they're in a group."

Becca continued. "But is it dating when Nate and I go together with you?"

"Yes." Hannah thought for a moment. "Because you two are more exclusive. Everyone knows you're together even when you're not with each other."

"And that's wrong?" Becca asked.

Hannah responded with a question of her own. "Do you think you're going to marry him?"

"Hannah, that's forever away! I'm 16!"

"But you're investing your heart in someone who may be meant for someone else. You're sharing intimate things about your life and becoming emotionally involved with him. How do you think your future husband would feel about that?"

"I doubt he's going to care. Nate and I haven't even kissed yet. Besides, I talk to you two about more stuff than I share with him. Would my future husband be hurt that I told deep secrets to Jacie?"

"Maybe we should stop sharing deodorant, too, Becca," Jacie said, straight-faced.

Becca bopped Jacie on the shoulder.

"It's true that Nate and I have some deep talks. But I wouldn't be able to really get to know him if all we talked about was the weather and the most recent Nuggets game. I think we have a healthy relationship, and so do my parents."

"But does God?" Hannah inquired.

Becca looked thoughtful. "I think so. I mean, He hasn't sent me a postcard saying otherwise. I'm not dependent on Nate and I don't put him at the center of my life. We don't cross lines—physically or emotionally."

"But how close to the lines do you get?"

"What do you mean?" Becca and Jacie spoke simultaneously.

"You're careful not to cross the lines, but isn't that like telling God, 'I'm going to get as close to messing up as possible without actually sinning,' when instead we should be saying, 'I want to get as far from sin as I possibly can.' Remember that the Bible says to flee temptation, not walk right up to it."

Becca tossed her paper plate in the trash. "But that doesn't mean we hide in caves with our Bibles. We still need to relate to other people. We still need to trust other people. God created us for relationships. And sometimes that's a risk."

"But if your body and heart belong to God, then are they really yours to take risks with?" Hannah remained calm, but the question was pointed.

Jacie and Becca exchanged glances.

"Listen, Hannah," Becca began. "We really respect your convictions about courtship. That takes a lot of discipline—"

"A *lot*," piped up Jacie.

"But we don't necessarily believe that it's the only way to go," Becca continued.

"It's the godliest way to go," Hannah countered.

"I'm not even sure about that," Jacie said. "I think there's such a thing as godly dating, too. If you're still sticking to God's guidelines about purity and are committed to following Christ—"

"And listening to and obeying God when He puts something on your heart." Becca deepened her voice to do her best God impression: " 'This guy isn't right for you, Becca. Break it off.' "

"But wait a second. Jacie just mentioned purity," Hannah said. "Wouldn't purity at its best be not dating at all?"

"Not necessarily," Jacie said. "What about like Becca and Nate—going out for dinner together, or hanging out with friends or doing youth group stuff?"

"Without being majorly exclusive or physical," Becca added. "Nate and I have a really good friendship, and that's the foundation of our relationship. We pray for each other, talk about what God's doing in our lives, and encourage each other in our walk with Him."

"It never talks about dating in the Bible, though," Hannah reminded her.

"It doesn't talk about courtship either," Becca said, her frustration beginning to get the better of her.

"But who says it didn't exist?" Jacie asked, trying, as always, to diffuse the tension. "Maybe Adam did take Eve out for coffee."

"Or for a rib sandwich." Becca laughed at her own joke. "The thing is, Hannah, courtship may be great for some people—"

"Like you, for example," interjected Jacie.

"But for other people, Christ-centered dating might be just as good," finished Becca.

"And sometimes you come across as judgmental when you talk about it," Jacie said, trying to be gentle.

"All I'm doing is proclaiming the truth," Hannah argued, "which the world doesn't care about. But I'll keep doing it anyway." She sighed, softening her tone. "I don't mean to come across as judgmental. But I worry about what these relationships will do to you. They're dangerous."

Becca blew a frustrated sigh upwards, scattering her bangs. "Hannah, you sound like you're talking about drug dealing. I love you to pieces, but you're way too scared about guys."

"I'm not so sure about that. She seemed to be having a pretty comfortable chat with Brendan on the bus ride up here," prodded Jacie, hinting for more details on the conversation.

Hannah bit her lip. Had people noticed? Her mind flashed back to the question about Tyler that had been brought up in health class. What would those people think if they had seen her with Brendan? *At this rate I'm never going to convince anyone about courtship.*

Becca jumped in, less subtle as usual. "Yeah. I noticed that, too. He's pretty cute, Hannah. What do you think of him?"

"Well, he's my editor. Of course we had to talk. It's my first assignment."

"That's funny," Jacie said. "I didn't notice any talk about camera angles or film developing."

"I wasn't close enough to hear," Becca said, "but if that was the topic of conversation, it's funnier than I ever thought it would be. You were laughing your head off, Hannah."

"I was not." She paused. "He was just being nice to me. He wants me to feel part of the team. That's part of his job." Saying it out loud somehow made it easier to believe.

• • •

In the world, not of it.

Hannah kept repeating the phrase in her head. She looked up at the clock again. 11:07. She had been trying to fall asleep for over an hour.

Solana was still out with Marcus. Every time Hannah heard footsteps in the hall she would wait for the door to open. But they always kept going. She said yet another quick prayer for Solana's safety. Could the girls be right? What an awful mistake for Solana to make! Hannah knew Solana would regret her actions forever. Maybe *she* should have said something to Solana. Oh . . . who was she kidding? Solana wasn't open to hearing stuff like that.

Hannah remembered her prayer on the bus. Maybe God had put her and Solana in the same room together so they could talk about courtship . . . maybe. If only Solana knew how much better her life could be—if she only understood how precious her purity was.

Courtship took on a whole new meaning for Hannah on her 13th birthday. She remembered the day clearly. Her mom had said they were going to have a ladies' day. The two of them went out for breakfast, and then shopping at the mall for her first bra. Over lunch Mrs. Connor had told her about how much she and her dad loved her and how they knew she must be getting curious about boys. She told her that they wanted to protect her from making a mistake by getting into a relationship too soon or not waiting for "the one God intended for her." It was then that Hannah's mom explained the process of courtship to her. Hannah had felt very grown up as they discussed such things. She wanted to be the "responsible young lady" her mom kept referring to. Until that day she had only been a girl; now she was a "lady."

That evening, after her favorite meal of tacos and rice, the family had cake and ice cream while she opened presents. The last gift was from her parents—a small box wrapped in gold paper. She opened it carefully—like a responsible young lady would, she supposed. Inside was her promise ring. A delicate gold band with her birthstone mounted on top. She stared at the beauty of the transparent aquamarine, the blue-greens shifting and sparkling under the light. It had been a very "lady-like" gift. Her mother explained that this was a symbol of the promise of purity they had talked about earlier that day, and she should wear it on the ring finger of her left hand until it was replaced by an engagement ring.

An engagement ring. That seemed like a long way off. Which was fine with Hannah. She had placed the promise ring on her finger *never* wanting to take it off. Sometimes when she was nervous, she would twist it around her finger. And she found herself doing it now.

She looked at it by the dim bathroom light she had left on for

Solana. The ring still sat daintily on her finger, the stone sparkling in the light.

Hannah lowered her hand, rolling over on the bed to turn away from the light. *Where* is *Solana?*

She shut her eyes. *God, You must have brought me here for a purpose. Was it to impact Solana? Is there anyone else to whom You want me to talk about courtship?* She considered people she had spoken with during the day. Brendan's lively expressions flitted through her mind. *That was a great conversation.*

She smiled to herself.

And then her smile faded.

I didn't say anything about courtship.

Or even God.

• • •

The sound of the door opening jolted Hannah upright. Solana looked surprised to see Hannah staring at her, the bathroom light still on.

"You didn't have to wait up," Solana said, sounding defensive.

"I know. I was just . . . worried." Hannah hesitated to admit it. Solana thought she was weird enough without her acting like a paranoid mother.

"You don't have to be worried about me." Solana stepped into the bathroom. "I can take care of myself."

"I know, but I'm concerned that you might make some mistakes," Hannah called over the rushing water.

The water shut off.

"Listen, Hannah." Solana's eyes were on fire as she stepped out of the bathroom, hands on her hips. "This weekend will be long enough with the two of us in here. Let's not make it an eternity. Do me a favor and save the lectures for someone else."

Hannah immediately knew she'd made a mistake. "Solana, honestly,

I'm not trying to pass judgment on you—"

"Really? 'Cause it sure seems that way."

"I think you deserve better."

"Like maybe some Bible-thumping preacher's kid with greased hair and a pocket protector? No thanks."

"Most Christian guys aren't like that at all. In fact—"

"Relax, Hannah." Solana halted her protest with an upraised hand. "I'm just being sarcastic. You don't need to defend all the boys in your Sunday school class."

"I only mean you deserve someone who appreciates you for who you really are. Beyond your face and your figure—someone who recognizes that you're funny and intelligent and talented."

Solana's face softened a bit. The fiery eyes smoldered. But fight remained edged into her voice. "You're just saying that."

"Solana, there are a lot of things you may not like about me, but you've been around me enough to know that I don't make stuff up. You are one of the smartest people I know. Seriously, I've never seen *anyone* who's such a whiz at science. You can have incredibly intelligent conversations, but you always end up with these guys who only care about . . . anatomy." Hannah thought that was the safest way to explain it.

Solana appeared thoughtful. "Thanks, Hannah. In some ways you're right."

The girls looked at each other, not knowing what to say next.

Maybe Solana is closer to giving her heart to God than I think. If she could see how her lifestyle and the way she dresses attracts guys like that, maybe she would change. She might even realize how having God in her life can keep her from acting that way.

"Y'know, it might help if you dressed a bit more modestly."

Solana sighed and rolled her eyes. "Don't push your luck." But she smiled as she walked back into the bathroom.

chapter 10

Hannah stood next to Brendan, her ski poles plunged into the packed snow. He said nothing, his gaze sweeping across the jagged peaks in front of them. "What are you thinking?" she finally asked.

"Psychopath," Brendan said, his voice certain.

Hannah stared at him. "That was rude," she said.

"What?" Brendan's brows furrowed in confusion.

"Why did you call me a psychopath?"

Brendan tipped his head back and laughed louder than she'd ever heard him laugh. She put her hands on her hips and waited for him to stop.

"It's the name of the ski run," he said, waving his hand toward the enormous mountain right in front of them. "It's the best black diamond run at Breckenridge—maybe even in all of Colorado!"

"Black diamond? What does that mean?"

Brendan looked at her and grinned, as though he thought she were joking around. But seeing her blank face, he did a double take. "You're serious?"

"I've never really skied before." Hannah stared down at the powdery snow wisping across her skis, afraid of what his reaction would be. The key word was "really." Her family had gone once in Michigan, but it wasn't anything like this. The reality had hit home when she woke up and looked out her window. Seeing the slopes in broad daylight dropped her stomach somewhere around her knees. These mountains were huge. She had known skiing would be more intense in Colorado, but she hadn't prepared herself for this. The bunny slopes here were literally the size of the most advanced slopes in Michigan. She could already feel her palms sweating inside her mittens.

"You know, you might have mentioned your lack of skiing experience before," chastised Brendan. But there was a smile in his voice.

Hannah looked up to see that his eyes were laughing, and it looked like he was doing all he could to keep the rest of him from doing the same.

"A black diamond run is among the most difficult," he told her. "The runs are rated by a diamond system with the easiest being green, and the most difficult being a double black diamond."

"And you're taking me up a *black* diamond run?" Hannah attempted to sound casual but her voice squeaked in the middle.

Brendan shrugged. "This is a *ski* club. I presumed you knew how since you didn't say anything when I asked you to take the pictures."

"I didn't think it would be such a big deal." She took a deep breath. "I knew I wouldn't be able to ski like the rest of you, but I thought the photos would all be done on smaller slopes, or even down here on the ground."

Brendan's laughter escaped. "There's still ground up there, Hannah. It's just a little higher ground."

"I know." Hannah knew she was embarrassing herself. "What about taking pictures at the lodge? I noticed that there's a skylight by the fireplace which would provide optimum lighting." She bit her bottom lip and looked up at Brendan, hopeful that he would change his mind. By the look on his face she knew—*no such luck*. She corrected her thought. *No, I mean blessing*.

"The ski team can't have their picture taken *inside*. You're going up that mountain, Hannah. I'm making sure of it."

"It's not the going up that concerns me." Hannah stared at her long skis. "It's the coming down part that bothers me more. I mean, these skis are so awkward. It took me almost a half an hour to get from the ski rental place to here," she said.

Brendan rested his hand on her shoulder. "I'll make sure you get down in one piece. I guarantee it." He stroked the bottom of her chin with his gloved thumb, causing her face to look up into those amazing brown eyes. "Okay?"

Hannah felt off-balance, wobbling on the edge of her skis. Her chin and shoulder burned where Brendan touched her. She had lost her voice in her stomach, so she just nodded. She believed he would take care of her. And she was more than happy to let him.

A black blur passed Hannah, spinning in one quick movement, spraying snow on them both. A gloved hand lifted goggles over a black ski cap. Tyler grinned at Hannah. "Wanna go on a run with me? I promise we'll take it easy."

Brendan answered before Hannah had the chance. "Sorry, Jennings. Hannah has a job to do. We're heading up to take pictures on Psychopath."

"Psychopath?" Tyler's lighthearted expression transformed to concern. "Hannah, are you sure you want to do that?"

Brendan jumped in again. "You're scaring her, Jennings. She'll be fine. We'll take it slow on the way down, and I'll be with her every step of the way." Brendan stood at Hannah's side and put a possessive hand on her shoulder.

Hannah nodded again. *I need to say something*, but Brendan's touch made her head swim. "I'll be fine, Tyler," she managed to blurt out.

"Do you want me to come up with you, too. I could—"

Brendan cut him off. "There's no reason you should miss out on a whole morning of skiing. One of us is enough."

Hannah couldn't help but notice the emphasis that Brendan placed on that last sentence.

"Okay," Tyler said. "Don't forget about our dinner plans, Hannah. I'll see you tonight."

Hannah shifted uncomfortably. She noticed that although Tyler's words were directed at her, his eyes bored into Brendan's. Brendan stared back. Without waiting for a response, Tyler lowered his goggles, made another quick turn, and skied away.

Hannah watched him go, wondering why the two boys didn't seem to get along.

"Let's go," Brendan said, touching her elbow, a quick jerk of his head toward the ski lift.

"It looks like fun," Hannah said.

"Not as fun as when the wind blows and makes those seats sway. It's a great carnival ride."

They moved slowly through the snow, Hannah finding that with every step forward she slid two steps back. Brendan gave her some hints that helped her do better. By the time Hannah made it to the lift, she felt she'd gotten the rhythm down.

As they stood in line for the lift, the sun warmed them. Brendan asked twice if she was wearing sunblock. "You wouldn't think you'd need sunscreen in the winter, but the sun reflects off the snow, making it even more intense. I learned the hard way." He gave her a wink, then guided her into the space in front of the advancing chair.

Hannah gasped as the slow-moving ski lift jolted her off her feet. *What were people thinking when they made this thing?* The ground moved farther and farther away. She stared at the ground, wishing to be back on it. Instead, she was perched on a narrow seat with nothing between her and a quick fall to her untimely death. A multitude of faceless ski jackets topped with knitted caps sped by underneath her. She held her breath as the skiers dodged the tall pines.

"I can't wait for my first run of the season." Brendan's bright eyes danced at the prospect. "Look behind you!"

Are you crazy? Hannah thought. But she grasped the metal bar at her side, carefully twisting her head around. "Wow! I see what you mean."

The quaint little cobblestone village seemed a mile away, covered under a blanket of snow. Wisps of smoke curled into the deep blue sky. And high above, framing the picturesque scene, stood the majestic Rockies. The sharp, frosted summits were both striking in their beauty and intense in their power.

Below her, bright sunlight illuminated smaller white peaks nearby, interrupted only by rocky crags casting long shadows. Since moving to Colorado, Hannah had loved looking up at the mountains, but she had never looked *down* at them. It was incredible!

"Pretty amazing, isn't it?" Brendan swung his legs with the excitement of a child.

Hannah gulped as their precarious seat began to sway.

"Oh, I'm sorry," he said, noticing her concern. If she wasn't so frightened, Hannah would have enjoyed Brendan's temporary break from poise to little boy.

"That's okay," she assured him, her confident words contrasting with her tiny voice.

The seats ahead began disappearing over a snow-covered ledge. *Finally, the end of the line*, Hannah thought with relief. As they cleared the ledge, she saw the lift continued up the mountain—she couldn't even *see* the end of the line. She groaned.

"Are you okay?" Brendan looked concerned.

"How much longer are we going to be on this?"

Brendan glanced at his watch. "We're almost there. The ride is about 15 minutes long. I told everyone to meet at 10:00. I hope they don't have to wait for us."

The end of the ski lift appeared in the distance. "Hand me the camera bag, Hannah. Now hold onto my arm and stand up when I tell you to. When you stand up, we're going to veer to the right. Okay?"

All of a sudden the ski lift seemed to be going much faster. Her skis looked bigger and more awkward. It felt like she was trying to maneuver with five-foot-long drapery rods tied to her feet.

Watching the people getting off in front of them calmed her. It looked easy enough. They just stood up and slid down the little slope. *But what if I don't get off in time? What if I miss the turn and get off late and drop 30 feet to the snow below? What if I end up riding the ski lift all the way back down again?* She smiled to herself. *Maybe that's not such a bad idea.*

"Hold tight," Brendan said. Hannah strengthened her grip on his forearm and noticed too late that as she did, she let go of her ski poles. She watched helplessly as the two poles fell to the snow below, making a black **X** on the white background.

She bit her lip and turned to Brendan. "Oops." *What do I do now?* she wondered.

Brendan grinned. "You really are going to be quite the adventure, aren't you?"

"What do I do?"

"We'll just pick them up on the way down." He patted her hand still gripping his bicep. "Don't worry about it."

Hannah wasn't sure what to do with his affection. Part of her wanted to jump off the seat to escape it. But deeper down, she almost wished they could ride on the ski lift up and down all day with Brendan's hand on hers.

"Hold tight . . . now . . . stand up." The feeling of slippery ground moving under Hannah took her by surprise. She tried to stand but fell backward. As she tried to regain her balance, her skis veered to the left.

Right, go right, she willed her skis, which were anything but obedient. *I can't watch this*, she thought, scrunching her eyes shut. She dug her fingers into Brendan's arm, trusting him to get her to where they needed to go. But her skis moved without her permission, twisting her body so her feet turned the wrong direction. Her back arched, her head slowly getting closer to the snow.

Brendan somehow managed to stay upright and stopped. Hannah opened her eyes, only to find she was looking up at the sky. Both hands were wrapped tightly around Brendan's arm. A ripple of applause from a world of upside-down faces greeted them.

"Never saw a lift dismount quite like that, Hannah," she heard a familiar voice say. "I give it a 9.5." She had a distorted view of Marcus McAllister's face flashing a cocky grin. She smiled back and let go of Brendan's arm. She twisted herself around, forgetting that the skis attached to her feet would hinder easy turning. She landed in a heap.

"Are you okay?" asked Brendan with concern.

"I'm fine," she said. *Besides being completely humiliated on my first day on the job*. She busied herself by brushing the snow out of her long ponytail.

Brendan helped her up, letting his hands linger on her arms. "I think you're better than fine." He squeezed her shoulders. "Knock 'em dead."

Once Hannah regained her composure, she looked around for where she'd set up the photo shoot. Despite her initial resistance to the idea, she had to admit the backdrop was incredible.

Now that she was in her element—comfortable behind the camera—the photo shoot went well. Arranging the 15-member ski team didn't seem all that different from arranging her family of eight for their annual Christmas photograph. She expertly moved people around, taking full advantage of the light.

Even as she went about her work, her mind wandered. She didn't like where it went, but she seemed unable to stop it. *What had Brendan meant when he said, "I think you're better than fine"?*

Click.

"Move that way just a little. Good."

Click.

Just a pep talk, I'm sure. He's probably scared to death I'm going to humiliate the newspaper and knew I needed the encouragement.

"Okay, everyone do something silly. Great! Hold it!"

Click. Click. Click.

But . . . what if . . . what if it wasn't about my photography skills? What if he meant something more? Of course he didn't. She mentally scolded herself for even allowing her thoughts to wander there. *He's just being encouraging. He doesn't want me to mess up this assignment.*

"Just one more," she said, changing her filter. "The sun's moving and we're getting some glare. This time, can Jayna and Katie kneel down in front with the others? And, Kyle, shift to the right—you're in a shadow. Knees the other way, Katie. Thanks. Get in close. Okay . . . one, two, three."

Click.

"That's it, everyone."

The group clapped and scattered. Marcus got their attention and gave instructions for the rest of the day. Brendan slid up next to her. *There it goes again*, she thought to herself, feeling her heartbeat getting faster and faster.

"You're quite the professional," he said, impressed. "Nice job."

"Thanks." Hannah smiled. "It was a piece of cake compared to trying to shoot rambunctious four-year-olds."

"Don't downplay it. You did great. They're not an easy crew to keep focused."

Hannah grinned up at him.

"No pun intended," he added.

"I enjoyed it." Hannah started latching her boots back onto her skis. Now it was back to the unfamiliar.

"I could tell. Are you ready for the downward trek?"

Hannah took a deep breath. "I guess so. But can I do it without poles until we pick them up?"

"Sure, it's better to learn without poles, anyway. Otherwise, you depend on them too much. Poles are primarily for turning, but new skiers often use them for balance."

"I'm glad you know what you're doing."

As Brendan guided her toward the edge of the run, Hannah realized how much she meant that last statement. She was about to begin one of the scariest moments in her life, and yet she felt safe and protected with him there. It was a good feeling.

chapter 11

The trip down the steep mountain was more fun than Hannah had expected. After a tense start, and feeling like a moron while Brendan retrieved her poles, she began to relax. She could laugh at her frequent falls and the times she ran into wiped-out snowboarders—also a common occurrence.

"Snowplow!" Brendan called after her when she got out of control, encouraging her to make a wedge with her skis.

"I'm trying, but it turns me around," Hannah laughed, sliding backward on the seat of her snow pants.

"I'm beginning to think you're doing this on purpose," Brendan said, extending his hand to her for the sixth time. "You just want to see if chivalry is still alive."

Hannah playfully slapped his hand away. "Forget you! I'll get up by myself." She struggled to get up on the slippery skis but couldn't quite make it.

"Give up?" he asked, crossing his arms.

She stuck out her mittened hand. "Okay, you win."

As they navigated the more steep and narrow areas of the trail, the two agreed that Hannah shouldn't even try to steer. Instead, she would shout to the other skiers, "I can't ski!" and hopefully they would move out of her path in time.

Hannah began a pattern of ski and fall, ski and fall, with the falling becoming less frequent. "Hey, I'm starting to get the hang of this!" she yelled back at Brendan, right before she felt her skis slip beneath her. She overcompensated by leaning too far forward and dove face-first into the soft snow. Brendan skied up behind her after picking up the discarded skis.

"I can tell," he said, laughing. He plopped down next to her and waited for her to put them back on.

"It wasn't totally my fault. There were a bunch of bumps back there. Someone should smooth those out."

Brendan grinned at her, handing her the other ski. "They're called moguls, and they're supposed to be there."

"Oh."

"But I have to admit, I've never seen anyone go over moguls on their stomach. I mean, I've heard of bodysurfing, but you're a natural at body-skiing."

Hannah laughed. "Why be like everyone else?"

She couldn't believe how natural it felt to be with Brendan. She had always felt guarded and uncomfortable with other guys—well, except with Tyler, of course, but he didn't count. Usually, she would do everything she could to avoid spending one-on-one time with a boy.

Hannah squinted up at the sun, wondering what her parents would think of this. She would have to tell them. Would they be disappointed? But what choice did she have? She had to go up there for the pictures, and she certainly had to get back down again. Should she have asked Tyler to come, too? He seemed willing enough, and then she could have avoided being alone with Brendan. But she sensed from the brief conversation that morning that there was some tension between the two boys. Should she have asked one of the girls on the ski team to help her down instead? She hardly knew any of them, and it would have been unfair to ask them to miss out on their skiing in order to baby sit her. She felt torn. Part of her knew this was so wrong—these feelings, this enjoyment of being with a boy. But the rest of her was enjoying it too much to even think about how wrong it might be.

"What are you thinking about?" Brendan's deep voice broke into her mental deliberation.

Hannah thought fast. "I was just thinking about how much I appreciated your patience with me. I know this has taken up a lot of your time." That was true—it wasn't the whole truth, but it was true.

"Trust me, Hannah. I've had a lot of fun doing this. You've been a great sport."

"Thanks. And you've been a great teacher." She looked at him out of the corner of her eye.

He scooted closer to her. Hannah felt the panic rise up in her. What was he doing? She began to frantically fumble with her ski.

"I can't get this ski on. I wonder if the binding broke on that last tumble."

"You might try turning it around. You're putting in on backward," said Brendan.

"Oh . . . yeah." To Hannah's relief, the uncomfortable moment was broken. But her corresponding disappointment surprised her. *Help me be strong, God.* She remembered her thoughts as she lay in bed last night. Now would be a perfect time to bring up God.

"It's so beautiful here I can't get over it." She looked around at the snow-covered scenery.

"Very beautiful," he agreed. But his eyes weren't on the scenery. They were fixed on her.

Hannah fought to stay on the subject. "I don't understand how people can't believe in God when they see places like this. Can you?"

"It sure makes more sense than evolution," he said.

One point for Brendan.

"We had a speaker at church—my old church back in Michigan—who talked about the whole creation-versus-evolution debate. And he had tons of proof on why evolution doesn't make sense." She looked over at him to watch his reaction.

"I remember hearing a speaker like that once, too. It was at some youth rally."

Another point.

"Are you really involved in your youth group?" Maybe he even served as the youth group president. Her parents would love that!

"Not so much anymore. School just got so busy, especially now with the newspaper. But I go with my parents to church most Sundays." Brendan stood up, indicating he was done talking, and helped her to her feet. They continued down the slope, Hannah trying to concentrate on traversing with proper form and Brendan occasionally shouting out pointers.

The conversation hadn't been all that she had hoped, but she kept telling herself that it could have been worse. Hannah shoved the nagging guilt out of her mind and decided she would just enjoy the day.

The trees were casting longer shadows and the wind felt colder. *It must be around two o'clock*, she decided. Maybe Brendan's patience had finally reached its limit. She caught him glancing back up the mountain a couple times. *I bet he's thinking he could have done five runs in the time it took him to get me down one.*

"Hey, baby, lookin' good!" came a strange voice from behind her. A snowboarder wearing cut-off shorts and a ski vest swerved around her, cutting her off. Hannah, caught by surprise, leaned back and lost her balance.

The snowboarder hopped off his board. "Oh, I'm sorry. Can I help you up?"

"No," came Brendan's commanding voice from a few yards below them. "But you can start boarding a little more carefully, and think of a new way to pick up girls."

The boarder's cocky grin disappeared. "Oh, sorry, man. I didn't know she was taken." Hannah felt like she should correct him, but after a quick glance in Brendan's direction she knew he was handling it. The two guys exchanged nods, and the boarder continued down the slope.

"What was that all about?" Hannah asked.

"You're naïveté is absolutely charming," he said, smiling. "You don't even know you're beautiful, do you?"

Hannah didn't have any idea how to respond. 'No' sounded like she was asking him to assure her of his opinion. 'Yes' sounded arrogant. Did Brendan really think she was beautiful?

The snowboarder had said he didn't know she was taken. *Taken?* Brendan hadn't argued with that. Was that his way of trying to protect her, or did he really feel that way about her? Like he was attracted to her. Maybe he was considering asking her out sometime. What would it be like to date Brendan Curtis? To walk into a room on his arm, to stroll hand in hand along Stony Brook during lunch, to have him over to her house for dinner.

What am I thinking? Hannah realized she was staring at him—and, funny thing was, he was staring back at her. His brown eyes locked onto hers. She couldn't look away if she tried. But she certainly wasn't trying.

"Are you okay?" Although his voice was tender, his eyes searched hers with great intensity.

For about the 12th time that day, he helped her up. But this time she noticed his hands had moved down to her waist, where he tightened his grip. His arms circled her, but she didn't push away. She froze. She couldn't remember a time when she had so deeply wanted to be close to someone, and yet she knew she should be running the other way. But she didn't go anywhere. *This is so wrong. This is so wrong.*

Brendan's strong arms pulled her near him, and he bent his head down so their foreheads touched. She could feel his breath on her face. And then his mouth moved closer to hers.

Pull away, Hannah. You have to pull away. But instead she stood still—stiff except for her racing heart. Brendan's nose caressed the edge of hers. Every nerve in Hannah's body seemed to be standing on end. She didn't know what to do. She didn't know what he wanted her to do. The only thing she knew to do was the one thing she wasn't doing—pushing him away.

She became aware that she had been holding her breath since he first pulled her up near him. She exhaled quickly, letting out a nervous laugh. Brendan pulled his face away and smiled, looking deep into her eyes. *Was it over?* She longed for him to come close again. Really longed. As if reading her thoughts, he tucked one hand behind her head, with the other still on the small of her back, and in one smooth motion pulled her to him, connecting her mouth to his. Gentle, sweet, soft, and tender. A warmth rushed through Hannah that left her tingling. He pulled back slowly, brushing his lips across her forehead. He gave her his incredibly cute crooked smile and let his arms drop from around her, but he continued to stand there looking at her. Oblivious to the rest of the world, Hannah could only concentrate on what was in front of her face—the strong chin, the half smile, the deep eyes.

"Hey, Curtis. Where've you been all day?" The voice came from a group of guys who had come down a catwalk that joined the end of this run with another. To Hannah's relief, it appeared that the last turn would have kept them from observing the kiss.

"Skiing, of course," Brendan replied. *Calm and cool as usual*, Hannah noticed.

A boy she didn't recognize looked past Brendan and gave Hannah the once-over. "So I see," he said with a smirk. "Well, listen, man, there's a bunch of us going up to try some jumps. Are you up for it?"

Brendan glanced back at Hannah. "Are you okay?" He seemed genuinely concerned. "You're almost to the bottom."

Hannah could see the liftlines at the end of the slope. She hadn't realized they were so close to the end. All of a sudden, this eternal slope seemed way too short.

"Sure. Thank you for your help." She tried to sound as casual as he did, hoping to give the other guys the impression that this was merely an innocent ski lesson.

"You did great." He leaned in closer and whispered in her ear, "Really great."

The other boys shifted impatiently behind him.

"I'll see you later," he said, giving her a wink. And with that they took off.

Hannah watched his retreating yellow and blue jacket and exhaled the breath she had been holding. Her head was swimming with thoughts and questions. *What did I do? What does this mean? What was I thinking? What will my parents say?* But beneath all that, she could still feel his soft touch on her lips, still sense his fingers on the back of her neck, and still think . . . *hmmm, Hannah Curtis doesn't sound all that bad. I wouldn't even have to change the initials monogrammed on my towels.*

She giggled. She felt giddier than she had . . . well, ever. She eased her way down the end of the slope. Skiing was wonderful, the day was beautiful, and Brendan Curtis liked her—*really* liked her.

chapter 12

"I think we're a couple now." Hannah's statement came out more like a groan.

"A couple of what?" Solana asked with a smirk on her face.

"You know what I mean. We're . . . dating!" Hannah sat on the edge of her bed, her head buried in her hands. Her blond hair hung over her face, hiding her expression.

Becca sat across from her on Solana's bed. "So what did you think of the kiss?"

"I don't know what to think. I love it and I hate it and I just can't believe it."

"You're not the only one," Solana said under her breath.

"My life is in shambles," said Hannah.

Scenes from the last few hours rushed through Hannah's mind like a slide show. She was so disappointed in herself, yet she couldn't get the feeling of that kiss out of her mind. She waffled between self-contempt and absolute giddiness.

Jacie flopped her body across Solana's pillows and looked squarely at Hannah with a hint of a smile. "Y'know, it hasn't gone unnoticed that you have been trying without much success to somehow suppress that huge grin on your face. If this is what it's like when your life is in shambles, you should try it more often."

The phone rang and Jacie reached for it.

I can't believe I did this, and yet it seemed so perfect. I'm still shaking from it. But I promised myself that I wouldn't kiss until I was married. And I promised God. What must He think of me?

"Tyler wants to know if we're ready to go to dinner," Jacie whispered as she held her hand over the phone receiver.

"I can't," said Hannah.

Jacie relayed the message.

"He wants to know why not," Jacie whispered.

Hannah shrugged and looked at the other girls.

"Just tell him she's sick," suggested Solana in a hushed voice.

"But that would be lying," said Hannah.

"Well, what do you want me to tell him?" asked Jacie.

The truth. *That's the correct answer, at least*, Hannah thought. But the truth was she felt like a complete failure and wasn't in the mood to go out and have a good time. She knew she would be distracted, and she didn't want to have to explain why. She didn't want Tyler to find out. He would never look at her the same if he knew. What would he think of her then? But she knew she couldn't lie to him, either, and if she didn't go out with the group tonight, he would be asking a lot of questions later.

Jacie raised her eyebrows in Hannah's direction, indicating Tyler was still waiting for an answer. "Tell him I'll come," Hannah said.

"I guess she changed her mind, Ty. She's coming after all," Jacie said. Tyler must have asked if Hannah was feeling better because Jacie said,

"Yeah, something like that." They arranged for a time to meet down in the lobby, and Jacie hung up the phone.

"I'm glad you're going, Hannah," Jacie said. "I think it will help you take your mind off things."

"Yeah. I really didn't like the idea of you being holed up here all night by yourself, either," Becca added.

When they entered the loud pizza joint, though, Hannah immediately wished she were holed up in the hotel room. Smoke wafted over from the bar, where crowds of people sat around on tall stools, talking and taking swigs from their long-necked bottles. A heavy beat pounded from the speakers above while a short-skirted waitress escorted the five-some to a long table on the other side of the restaurant.

"Here ya go," she shouted over the music as she handed out the menus. The group knew they shouldn't expect attentive service tonight. As soon as restaurant servers saw high school kids, they knew they wouldn't be ordering drinks from the bar and gave up the idea of a decent tip.

"Do you really want to eat here?" shouted Hannah. This place epitomized everything that was immoral—the dancing, the flirting, the drinking, the music. Everything that her parents would hope she'd avoid on her weekend away. But she didn't want to be the prissy, uptight one again. It seemed like she was always the party pooper. Besides, she had pretty much given up her right to be wholesome after the stunt she had pulled today. "I mean, it's really loud."

"They say the pizza is the best in town," said Becca.

"But we just had pizza last night!" said Hannah.

"What's your point?" Becca smiled.

Hannah had to admit, the pizza was good. And as the group grew accustomed to hearing each other over the music, they were able to share ski stories from the day. It seemed that everyone had their embarrassing moments. Hannah was almost going to share her upside-down-dismount-from-the-chairlift story when she realized she didn't want to go anywhere near the topic of Brendan.

The girls laughed themselves to tears as Tyler shared how he had been mistaken as a ski instructor. He somehow ended up with a dozen or so young skiers following him around like little ducklings after their mother. Tyler had a way with telling stories, and Hannah laughed until she noticed his clownish expression suddenly sobering. Before she could turn around to see what had caught his attention, she felt a hand on her shoulder and recognized Brendan's cologne. He leaned in so close his cheek brushed against hers as he addressed the group.

"How are you guys doing tonight?" Brendan asked.

The others girls gave lighthearted responses and shot comforting looks at Hannah. His hand kept sending electric shock signals down her arm. *Is this what love feels like? I want to throw up.*

Marcus, who was with Brendan's group, moved to the other side of the table, pulled Solana out of her chair, and asked her to dance with him. The two moved over to the small, jam-packed floor by the bar.

Please don't ask me to dance, Hannah thought. She wasn't as concerned about her moral stance against dancing as she was about looking like an idiot in front of Brendan.

But she didn't have to worry. After a couple minutes of chitchat, he gave her shoulder a squeeze and told everyone he would see them later.

The group paid the bill and then decided to take a walk around the village. Solana, to no one's surprise, decided not to join them. She and Marcus were so intertwined on the dance floor that it would have taken too long to extricate her anyway.

The four stepped out into a cool, crisp night—a welcome change from the stuffy bar. Countless stars glittered overhead, and despite the mingling conversations of passersby, the streets seemed silent. The four walked along the cobblestone walkways, admiring the picturesque storefronts and the thousands upon thousands of white lights adorning the city. Everything seemed perfectly quaint, down to the intricate ice sculpture in the town square and the Celtic band playing Christmas tunes.

The four sat on a ledge to listen. Jacie and Becca continued their chatter about the day, and Tyler tossed in smart comments.

Hannah tuned out for a while, staring up at the mountains that were now merely shadows against the dark sky. Somewhere up there, she had kissed Brendan. Her first kiss of all time. She remembered his lips pressed against hers. The shocks shooting through her system. The feel of his breath on her skin.

Why in the world did I do that? Are we dating now? Should I expect him to talk to my father? Should I ask him to? But the thought of her parents made her stomach churn even more. What would she tell them? What would they think of her? She was supposed to be the good example to her little brothers and sisters. And, even worse, someday she would have to tell her husband-to-be that she had given her first kiss to another. It may even bring him to tears to realize that his future wife had not remained pure. *Unless it was Brendan*. But she didn't even know if he was a Christian! *Oh, what in the world did I do?*

The laughter of the other three broke into her thoughts. Tyler good-naturedly tossed his arms around the three girls, with Becca and Jacie on his right and Hannah on his left. Hannah tensed up under his arm and gently shook it off. She didn't want to be touched right now—not by anyone. She stood up abruptly.

"I'm pretty tired," she announced, adding a yawn for effect. "I think I'll head back to the room."

"Do you want us to come with you?" asked Jacie. Concern etched her face.

"No. I'm just going to take a hot bath and go to bed. I'll see you tomorrow. Thank you, though."

"We'll pick you up for breakfast at 7:30," said Becca. "Sleep well."

Hannah ambled back to the hotel, grateful for the reprieve and the time to think and pray. There was a nagging question replaying over and over in the back of her mind.

What if courtship isn't what's best?

She wondered if she *was* missing out by not dating. The mere touch of Brendan's hand on her shoulder earlier that night had felt so right—so good. Marriage, at this point in her life, seemed so far off. How could she wait that long? How could she make Brendan wait that long?

I shouldn't have let him kiss me.

Would dating be such a horrible thing? She remembered wondering only a few days ago if she could trust that her mom and dad knew what was best. And now she questioned their judgment on this issue as well.

• • •

Hannah almost didn't hear the phone ringing over the gush of warm water filling the bathtub. Shutting off the water, she scrambled to get the phone. Tyler's voice came over the line before she could finish saying, "Hello."

"We need to talk," he said.

"Now?"

"Yes. I'll meet you in the lobby in 10 minutes."

Hannah grabbed her clothes to get redressed. She had almost told him that she couldn't talk tonight and asked if it could wait. But she couldn't dismiss the urgency in his voice. *What is this all about?* What if someone had said something to him—someone who saw her and Brendan together? She pulled her hair back in a bun. Maybe he was going to confront her about it. *As a brother in Christ should*, she said to herself. *I'll tell him I see the error of my ways.*

• • •

"Hi." Tyler was already waiting downstairs when Hannah got off the elevator.

"Hi. What did you want to talk about?" If this was going to sting, she'd rather just get it over with.

"Can we go for a walk?"

Under normal circumstances, Hannah wouldn't agree to walk alone with a boy, especially at night. But Tyler was different. Besides, he seemed so troubled. *And if this is about me and Brendan, I want to make sure we have complete privacy*. The last thing she needed was for someone to hear this conversation and repeat it in Monday's health class.

The two walked around the outside of the hotel until they came to a large outdoor fireplace. Since no one else was around, Tyler pulled two cushioned chairs close to the fire and motioned for her to have a seat.

Tyler wrung his hands and stared at his feet. He shifted in the chair and cleared his throat. He looked at her, then toward the fire. He took a deep breath and got right to the point. "Are you upset with me?"

"Upset with you?" Hannah didn't know what to say. "Of course not."

"Are you sure? Because I felt really bad about what happened at the Copperchino the other day. And . . . well, you seemed so distant tonight. So I thought you were still upset about that."

"I'm sorry, Tyler. Honestly. I'm not angry with you." She searched through scenes in her memory for what would make Tyler think she was upset with him. *It has to be my distraction with Brendan. But then, I guess Tyler's right. We haven't talked—*really *talked—in days.*

Hannah stared into the dancing orange flames. The friendship meant enough to Tyler that he was willing to face something difficult head-on in order for it to go back to normal. *How sweet of him to be concerned.*

She turned to look at him. "Tyler, you've been so amazing to me. You've included me in the Brio shoots, stood up for me when the rest of the group gave me a hard time, even sacrificed your plans for Homecoming because I couldn't go. And, of course," she blushed, "you rescued me when my bicycle tire was stolen. You've been a wonderful brother in Christ."

Tyler had his head down, tapping a foot and nodding, looking totally embarrassed.

Look at him. Because I was distracted with my own life, Tyler feels our friendship is declining. Hannah felt horrible that she had hurt him. She knew she could trust him. *I need to talk to* someone *about Brendan. Why not Tyler?*

Hannah debated about how much she should tell him. She didn't want to name names, but he did deserve to know she was struggling. And the Bible says Christians are supposed to share their burdens with each other. *This certainly qualifies.* "I'm just confused right now."

He looked at her with great concern. "What about?"

He cares so much.

Hannah took a deep breath. "I don't quite know how to say this, Tyler. It's kind of embarrassing, and I'm afraid of what you'll think of me." She paused momentarily and focused her gaze on the glowing embers. "But I could use your prayers to help me overcome it."

"Of course. I'll help in any way I can."

"Well, you know how I believe in courting?"

"Yes."

"And courting means that you save yourself physically and emotionally for the one you're going to marry."

"Right." None of this was new to Tyler, and she could tell he was anxious for her to move on.

"I've been having strong feelings for someone. A friend of mine. A boy. And I know I shouldn't feel this way. But I do."

There was a long silence. Hannah opted not to tell him about the kiss. *Some things shouldn't be shared in mixed company*, she decided. Besides, that was just a result of the sinful thought. An unimportant detail. The real struggle was the attraction.

"How do you feel . . . exactly?" asked Tyler.

"Really attracted to him. I feel so stupid saying this. I've always thought that I'd only be attracted to the man who would become my husband."

"You've never been attracted to *any* guy before?"

Hannah felt her cheeks grow warm. "Not like this. I mean, I've thought guys were cute before, but the attraction was never so overwhelming." Her voice drifted off as she spoke her thoughts aloud. She suddenly heard what she said. "I mean," she corrected herself, "it's not that I'm not controlling myself, it's just . . . difficult."

"Do you ever think of not courting?" asked Tyler. She noticed his voice had a higher pitch to it than usual.

How can he read my thoughts? How would he know that? She debated whether she should admit it or not.

"Sometimes. Sometimes, I wonder if it's really what's best. Or if I'm just missing out," she said softly. Even though they were her own words, hearing them out loud took her off-guard.

"Does . . . this guy . . . like you?"

Hannah closed her eyes for a split second, feeling Brendan's tender, warm lips on her own. The dancing in her stomach started again.

"I think so," she said. "But I don't know how to respond to it." She shook off her dreamy-sounding voice, remembering her earlier dilemma. "And I want to please God, too."

Hannah heard Tyler take a deep breath. She still couldn't look at him. "I bet it's really hard to be around him," he said.

"It is pretty awkward," she admitted. *Tyler really understands well*, she thought. And it felt good to talk about it. "I want to avoid him and be around him at the same time. Especially when I get those electric shock feelings."

"Yeah, I know what you mean," said Tyler.

"You do?" She felt so relieved.

"Yeah, I do."

There was another long silence. Hannah relished the warmth between friends.

"Hannah?"

She turned toward him, surprised at how close he was. The fire reflected in his eyes, making them light up. His strong jaw was only inches away.

"Yes?" she said, more breathily then she intended. She felt his hand on the back of her head, his fingers laced through her hair. The reflection of the fire cast waltzing shadows across his serious face.

"I feel the same way." He pulled her head toward him and his lips met hers in a strong kiss.

chapter 13

"You what?!" Jacie and Becca exclaimed in unison.

"Wow, even I've never kissed two different guys within a six-hour period," Solana said, nodding her approval.

This was no comfort to Hannah, however. She lay across her bed with her face buried in her pillow. "I'm a slut," she moaned, the words muffled.

How could you do this? her inner voice accused.

Still, she couldn't get the thought of Tyler's kiss out of her mind. Brendan's had been more gentle, but Tyler's had an unmistakable passion.

Look what happens when you question courtship—your whole world falls apart.

"Tyler must be flying high," Becca remarked.

"Yeah, until he finds out he's not the only one flying," added Jacie under her breath.

Hannah hated to think what she would have thought if she was hearing this story about someone else. She would have assumed that she was a user, and worse—a woman of unclean lips, loose, provocative.

But that's ME. Those things are ME.

She added voice to her thoughts. "I'm such a horrible person. God must hate me."

"Oh, Hannah, that's not true," Jacie said, going over to sit next to her. She put her arm around Hannah, who felt like pulling away.

I don't deserve kindness.

"Hannah, it may have been a mistake, but it's not an unforgivable sin," Becca added.

"Yeah," chimed in Jacie. "Everyone makes mistakes. Look at me."

Solana even revealed a rarely-seen softer side. "Is there anything we can do?"

"No. Thanks." Hannah heard their kind words, but she couldn't grasp them. It didn't feel like God could forgive her for this. She was supposed to be an example to her friends, a reflection of Christ, a witness to Solana. She was supposed to be pure. And she was anything but. "Can you guys go and leave me alone? I just want to go to bed."

"Sure," they said.

"I'll go with them," Solana said. "I'll be back later."

As soon as Hannah heard the door close behind them her tears started to fall.

• • •

Another sleepless night. She leaned against the pillow propped up behind her. Staring out the window, her mind drifting like the snowflakes she watched dance to the ground, as if playing some sort of game with one another.

They look just as confused as I am—but having a lot more fun.

When she first started school at Stony Brook, she had been an outsider because she was a strong believer. Now she was the outsider because she was the fallen believer. At least the snowflakes had each other. She was in this by herself. Who did she have to understand her?

I've always been able to put on a good Christian face pretty well. But when it comes down to it, I'm not much different than Solana, am I?

She rolled over, pulling the pillow over her head.

No, I'm even worse because I know better.

She took a deep breath.

God must be so disappointed with me.

Tears came to her eyes as she pictured Him up in heaven frowning down on her. She jammed the pillow harder on her head and mentally listed her failures she knew God must be listing, too:

I messed up the courtship speech.

I kissed Brendan.

I liked it.

I kissed Tyler.

I liked that, too.

Hannah flipped over and clenched her eyes shut tight, trying not to think about it anymore.

In the world, not of it.

The statement had been the running theme in her home. She'd heard it for as long as she could remember. But the first time it really affected her was when she was 10 and asked if she could paint her nails. The answer was no. Even now she didn't wear makeup, except for lip gloss. Her parents probably wouldn't care if she wore more now, but she knew Sarah Ruth and Rebekah would probably want to as well then. And she didn't want to put her parents in an awkward situation of explaining why Hannah was allowed to and they weren't. Besides, she'd gone 16 years without needing the stuff, why start now? Many of the girls at school put on so much makeup that they looked like they were dressed up for Halloween every day. *One less thing to take up time, one less thing to spend money on, one less thing to draw attention to myself.*

Hannah had always taken pride in her modesty. The leaders at church, particularly her former church back in Michigan, constantly held her up as a role model to the other kids.

Hannah, would you please recite our verse from last week? I know you'll remember it.

Now if everyone did their lessons as consistently as Hannah . . .

Hannah, why don't you share with Lizzie how you'd have handled that situation. You always know the right thing to say.

At first all the attention had pleased her. After all, in a family of six kids, you share a lot of the accolades—despite the fact that her parents were generous with their praise. But it didn't take her long to realize this also alienated her from the other kids. Some even resented her 'perfectionism'. And she began to feel more of the pressure. How could she mess up now that she had been put on this pedestal of being such a holy, good person? She would disappoint everyone. So she didn't wear makeup and she was careful to do her Bible lesson every week. She was afraid that someone would find out she wasn't at all the perfect person they believed her to be. Her parents had repeatedly reminded her not to be so hard on herself. But it was hard not to be. She was afraid of people finding out that she could be irresponsible or angry or vain.

Like the black dress.

Hannah scooted up and looked out the window again. But the falling snow disappeared as she pictured the secret garment. Back in Michigan she had been shopping for skirts in a thrift store when she noticed it—out of place on the skirt rack. At first she pushed right on past it. But then it caught her eye. It was made of layers of sheer, silky material, with a deep scoop neck, a fitted bodice, and a long, flowing skirt.

She lifted it, put it back, and lifted it again. There was nowhere she could wear it, but she decided to try it on anyway.

She slipped into the dressing room in the back of the nearly empty store and put it on. In order to see herself in the dress, she had to step outside the curtains. She had poked her head out and made sure no one was around before racing out to take a quick glance in the full-length mirror. The dress fit her perfectly—too perfectly. It fit and formed every curve. Her long leg escaped the slit from the thigh down. She stood staring at herself, almost in shock that this was actually her own reflection.

She twirled around, the silky layers swishing seductively around her bare legs. She posed in front of the mirror—her head cocked, one eyebrow raised, and a sultry smile on her lips.

"Wow!" A male voice behind her spoke. "You look incredible."

Hannah stiffened. She didn't want this man to see her. She didn't want anyone to see her. What if someone from church was there? She raced back into the changing room, and took a few deep breaths. How could she think like that? She was practically pretending to be some bar dancer or something. She rubbed her temples. The other nagging thought was that despite being horrified that she'd been seen, she enjoyed the man's compliment. *What is wrong with me?* Several minutes later she emerged, red-faced, with an armful of appropriately conservative clothes to purchase. The dress remained hanging in the small, curtain-covered changing room.

The voice she had heard belonged to the young man working the cash register. She avoided looking at him. As he folded her clothes, he didn't say anything. But before he placed her purchases in the brown paper bag, he walked over to the changing room and removed the dress, folded it, and placed it in the bag.

"I don't want that one," Hannah blurted out.

"I'm not charging you for it," he smiled and then continued his work. "No one else will look as perfect in it as you. Here's your receipt. Have a nice day."

She never went back to that thrift store.

But she did keep the dress in the back of her closet. On rare occasions she locked the door to her room, took it out, and put it on. She'd spin around in front of the mirror and watch the sheer layers fly. The dress still fit perfectly, *like a second skin*, she noticed with both admiration and disgust.

It's vanity, I know, she told herself. But she would still place it back on the hanger and hide it behind her winter coats—until next time. But it was more than vanity. She felt attractive, grown-up . . . yes, sexy, when she wore it. Solana had tried on a similar dress when the four girls went shopping last month. Hannah held back from giving her opinion, feeling like she would be hypocritical if she did. But it hadn't been necessary anyway. The other girls, Solana included, agreed it was too revealing.

"You know I like to advertise," Solana had quipped. "But there needs to be a little room left for imagination."

Maybe that's who I am, Hannah thought, bringing herself back to the present. *Maybe I'm really just the sleazy girl in a sexy black dress trying to live out a pretend life of innocence and holiness.*

She leaned her forehead against the cold pane. The snow swirled in a white blur.

I've messed up—big time. Both times. How can I go back to my commitment of purity? How can I say I'm someone who believes in courtship after what happened today?

What if courtship isn't even the answer?

As much as she tried to shove it out of her mind, she kept coming back to the feeling of Brendan's arms around her and the touch of his lips on hers. She tried to pray. Instead, she relived the intense kiss with Tyler—still feeling the warmth of the flames on her face.

She snuggled back under the covers again. Somewhere amid the tossing and turning, she finally drifted into a restless sleep.

Suddenly her mother appeared, handing her a piece of tiramisu and a mug of hot chocolate drenched in whipped cream. "Here you go, sweetie," she said.

"Thanks, Mom." Hannah looked around the room at each member of her family, each laughing and chatting with the others. All the kids were a few years older. The doorbell rang and she noticed her parents exchanging knowing glances. Dad lifted himself out of his recliner and went to answer the door. Hannah couldn't see who he was talking to in the other room, and he seemed to lower his voice so she couldn't make out what he was saying, either. Mr. Connor called her into the living room, and her mother followed behind, softly smiling in response to Hannah's questioning glance. She entered the living room, and there, with a bouquet of red roses, he stood.

"Hannah," her father began. "You remember Brendan Curtis?"

Hannah nodded. In her mind, she looked gentle and demure, a quiet smile on her lips.

"Brendan and I have been talking regularly over the last two years. Since he expressed his interest in you a couple of years ago, we have had a mentoring relationship," her father explained after the four of them sat down—she and her mother on the couch, with Brendan and her father in separate chairs across from them.

"Hannah," the young man said, "I would like to ask you if you would allow me to pursue you in courtship."

Something about his voice struck her as odd. She looked up at his face, closer now, and saw that it wasn't Brendan. It was Tyler.

"No!" Her own voice woke her up out of the dream, and she found herself sitting upright in bed, breathing hard. Solana lay in the next bed, her even breathing proof she had not been disturbed.

She collapsed back into bed. Eventually, she began going in and out of sleep again, visiting what seemed to be countless vignettes in fuzzy dreams: her dad skiing down the slope and looking disapprovingly at her in Brendan's arms, his angry vein throbbing in his forehead. The fire that she and Tyler had sat by crawling out and consuming her. Ms. Bennett announcing to the class what "Courtship Hannah" had done last weekend.

This is ridiculous, Hannah thought when she woke up from a dream in which she watched herself run around in a crowd of people with a piece of tape. She kept trying to find someone the tape would stick to, but as soon as she put it on someone, it would fall to the ground.

She looked at the clock. 5:24. As much as she wished the night would be over, she didn't want to face the day at all.

● ● ●

"I can't believe you're dragging me down there," Hannah complained as Becca hit the lobby button in the elevator. "I'll be absolutely humiliated."

"Well, you can't stay in the hotel room all day. So now's as good a time as any to face the world," Solana said.

"Why do I have to leave the room?"

"Because God was getting tired of you asking for forgiveness over and over again," said Solana, smirking. "Besides, we wanted to hear how Tyler kisses."

Becca covered her ears. "I don't want to hear this."

Hannah's eyes filled with tears. She leaned her head against the back of the elevator. "I can't believe this."

Jacie tried to be comforting. "It's not the end of the world, Hannah. I promise."

"I know." She wiped her eyes with her handkerchief. "I know God is still in control. I know He forgives. I know I should just face the day with a smile." She straightened up with renewed drive. "I'll be okay," she said with defiant determination.

The metal doors opened.

"I think," she added.

● ● ●

"Rooms 235 and 312," said Becca to the hostess. The students were supposed to give their room numbers, since their bills were already covered.

"235?" The young hostess smiled broadly. "Which one of you is Hannah?"

"I am, miss," said Hannah slowly. The other girls looked at her curiously.

"Well, you're a lucky girl." She leaned down behind the hostess stand and picked up a large glass vase filled with beautiful red roses. "A young man asked that I give these to you and wish you a good day." She handed the bouquet to Hannah and looked expectantly for her reaction.

Hannah just stood there, stunned. Her mouth open, barely hearing the gasps from her friends, she didn't know what to say.

"Thank you," she stammered out. "I need to go." She turned on her heel and headed back to the elevator.

She heard Solana's fading voice explaining her quick exit to the confused hostess. "She's just kind of anal about keeping the water changed . . ."

"Who are they from?" asked Jacie in a hushed tone as she caught up. Becca edged up on the other side.

"I don't know." Panic welled up inside her. What should she do? She held the flowers at arm's length, as if that would somehow make them go away. If they were from Brendan, what would she say to Tyler? If they were from Tyler, what would she say to Brendan? She would have to thank one of them—he'd expect it—but which one? Had either of them seen her get the flowers? She had to get upstairs before he stopped her.

Becca punched the up arrow, and Hannah tapped her foot impatiently, willing the elevator to hurry. He must have been watching. He, whoever he was, had come down early to give them to the hostess and was probably waiting to see her reaction. He was almost certainly coming to see what was wrong. She had to escape.

Ding.

The elevator arrived. Hannah breathed a sigh of relief as the doors opened.

Until her eyes met Brendan's . . . and Tyler's.

chapter 14

"Hi, Hannah," both boys said simultaneously.

Hannah stared at them. She tightened her grip on the vase of flowers, her mind racing to come up with some escape plan. They just looked at her; Brendan with an expression of amusement, Tyler concerned. Their expressions didn't help Hannah figure out the giver at all.

Why don't you do *something?* she screamed at them in her mind. *Someone say, "I see you got your flowers." Please!*

No, if he said that, then what would the other one do? Why didn't they get out of the elevator and go to breakfast? Maybe they didn't recognize her. Maybe she could pretend that she was some European tourist who just looked like Hannah Connor, while the real Hannah was up in her room with a headache for the next four days.

Oh sure. Like that will work.

She searched frantically for some escape but instead felt like a trapped animal—with five pairs of eyes watching for her next move.

Play it calm.

Ding!

The doors to a second elevator slid open. Hannah popped in, dodging the guests attempting to exit. She pushed the "2" button as the other girls quickly followed her lead, jamming themselves onto the elevator. The doors slid shut.

"You can't hide forever, Hannah," Becca said. "You'll need to talk to them sometime."

"I know, I know." She buried her face in the mass of perfect roses. "But I need time to figure out what I'm going to do first."

Becca wasn't done being practical. "You're not going to find a verse about this one, Hannah." She stared up at the numbers above the door. "You're just going to have to follow your heart."

Hannah racked her brain as the girls wordlessly made their way back to the room, trying to prove Becca wrong and think of some verse that would apply. She wanted something to say to the girls. She especially wanted to show Solana that God always gives the right answer. He was her guiding light.

Who am I kidding? she thought. *God probably isn't even listening. Not after the mess I made.* Proverbs 15:29 came immediately to her mind: "The LORD is far from the wicked, but He hears the prayer of the righteous."

She grabbed her Bible off the bed stand and curled up in the chair by the window. It wasn't anything like her own wicker chair, but it would have to do.

"Do you want us to stay with you?" asked Jacie, sitting on the foot of the bed.

"No, I just want some time by myself," said Hannah, staring at the corner.

Becca leaned against the closed door. "We'll go down to eat breakfast, then. Do you want us to bring you anything?"

"No, thank you."

The girls exchanged helpless glances and began filing out. Jacie stopped halfway out the door. "If Tyler or Brendan asks about you, what should we say?"

Hannah paused. She hadn't thought about that. She closed her eyes a moment, thinking. Then she sighed. There was nothing to do but tell the truth and face them—eventually. She looked at Jacie. "Tell them I am fine and I will speak with them later," she said resolutely.

As soon as the door closed, the tears came. She wanted to run—and keep running—to get further from Brendan, Tyler, and her own stupid mistakes. But she knew she couldn't outrun mistakes.

She didn't even know where to start with her Bible, so she put it back on the bed stand. The warm tears drenched her face, dripped down her chin, and soaked her collar. She blew her nose and picked up her journal instead.

God, I know I've disappointed You. I've given in to the desires of the flesh and I'm so sorry.

Hannah wasn't certain what "the desires of the flesh" entailed, but her father talked about it all the time—especially when he referred to those sins that were unmentionable. Hannah thought this must qualify.

I don't know how You could forgive me for my moral failure, but I do come before Thee and humble myself at Your feet and pray for Your unending mercy on me. Please forgive my many sins. Forgive me for desecrating the witness that You wanted me to be, and please help my foolish actions not to impact the eternal salvation of those who have observed my immorality.

She continued to write in her best, most careful handwriting.

Forgive me for giving in to the temptations of the devil, and please protect me from his deceiving ways.

Hannah read it over, her heart aching and heavy with guilt. Would God honor her agony? Was she repentant enough? What was enough repentance, anyway? With all her heart and soul she was sorry she'd allowed her relationships with these two boys to go so far. She hoped God would honor that.

But what should she do about Tyler and Brendan? She knew that because Brendan kissed her, they were probably dating. But when she kissed Tyler, did that mean she was cheating on Brendan? Or was she dating Tyler now, too? Could you date two boys at once? It was all so confusing. There was no other choice but to start over with a clean slate. She began making a list:

1. *If at all possible I will not be alone with a boy.*
2. *As of today, I will keep my lips pure until my wedding day. This time I mean it.*
3. *I will memorize verses on*

purity and will repeat them whenever I feel tempted to act in impure ways.

4. I will write letters to both Brendan and Tyler apologizing for my behavior and explaining my beliefs and that nothi

A knock on the door interrupted her thoughts. Hannah pictured Jacie standing outside with a tray of orange juice and whole wheat toast, insisting that Hannah eat something. *Good. Then I can talk to her about what I've decided.* She swung the door open.

"Hi," Tyler said. He looked both hesitant and pleased.

Hannah guessed that she looked like she was going to wet herself. Without thinking, she slammed the door.

I can't believe I just did that.

Tyler pounded on the other side. "Hannah, we need to talk."

"I'll write you a letter," Hannah called through the door.

"This is ridiculous," Tyler moaned.

Hannah heard a bump that sounded like Tyler's forehead hitting the door.

He's right. She cracked the door open and peeked through the slit.

They looked at each other until Tyler broke the silence. "Uh . . . can I come in?"

"Sure—I mean, no!" Hannah practically shouted, remembering rule #1. "Let's talk out there." She slipped outside the door, careful not to let it close all the way behind her.

"Okay." Tyler looked confused but didn't question her. "I wanted to talk to you about last night."

"Let me talk to you first," she butted in before she lost her nerve. "What happened between you and me should never have happened. It was wrong of me. I've asked God for forgiveness and now I want to ask you for forgiveness."

"Okay."

"Do you forgive me?"

"Yes."

"Do you want me to forgive you?"

"Can I say something first?"

Hannah realized she was treating Tyler like she would Sarah Ruth when the little girl forgot to say grace before snacking on a sandwich. "Sorry," Hannah said.

"I really like you, Hannah—"

"I don't think we should be talking about this," she interrupted. A bellhop passed by and looked at them curiously.

"Just let me finish. I like you, but I know a relationship wouldn't work for us because of your—"

"Are you breaking up with me?"

"Breaking up?" Tyler looked confused. "We were never dating!"

"We weren't?"

"No. Did you think . . . ?"

"Never mind. What do you want to say to me?"

"Even though we're both Christians, we see things differently. I'm sorry for kissing you. After giving it a lot of thought, I know it shouldn't have happened. I really like having you as a friend, and I don't want to lose that."

Hannah stared at him wide-eyed. This wasn't what she'd expected.

Tyler continued. "I know you believe in courting. I thought somehow I could convince you to, I don't know, let it go or something." He stared down at his shoes. "I'm sorry for wanting to make you compromise your beliefs. It was unfair of me. And I respect them—I respect you—too much for that."

Hannah nodded, not sure of what to say. "Thank you," she said quietly. "I forgive you."

Tyler looked up again and searched her eyes. "I hope this won't change our friendship."

Hannah shook her head. "Of course not."

An awkward silence hung between them.

Her mind went back to the flowers that sat on the dresser. Now was as good a time as any to find out. "Did you get me the roses?"

Tyler's brow wrinkled. "No, I didn't. You mean you don't know who they're from?"

"Well, now I do."

"Brendan?"

Hannah nodded. She wasn't sure how much Tyler knew, but she didn't want to reveal too much.

"Be careful with him, Hannah. He's an okay guy, but he's—" Tyler stopped himself. "Just be careful," he finished.

Hannah watched Tyler saunter down the hall. She stepped back into her room, closed the door, and leaned the weight of her body against it. *Thank you, God. That went well. We understand each other. We forgave each other.*

Hannah fingered one of the rosebuds peeking out from the baby's breath. *Then why do I feel so disappointed?*

● ● ●

Becca, Jacie, and Solana piled into the room, finishing off cream cheese-covered bagels.

"What happened?" Jacie asked.

"Tyler said he was coming up here," Becca said, her eyes wide, eager to hear the story.

"Are the flowers from him?" Solana asked.

"They're from Brendan. I'm going to try to find him and talk to him now," Hannah said, zipping up her jacket.

"What are you going to say?" Becca asked.

"I'm going to tell him it can't work, at least not right now."

Solana flopped on her bed, licking the cream cheese off a finger. "For some reason I don't think you believe that."

The truth struck Hannah hard, but she ignored it, walking out the door.

● ● ●

"Brendan! Can we talk for a minute?" Hannah called out when she caught sight of him in his yellow and navy jacket.

Brendan turned around and flashed Hannah one of his killer smiles. He waited for her to catch up.

"You can't ski in those," he said, pointing with one of his poles to her tennis shoes. He sounded serious, but his wink gave him away.

"I need to talk to you." Hannah kept her gaze steady, trying to appear emotionless. She wasn't counting on those eyes having the effect they were having right now.

"Sure. But can it wait until later? My friends are waiting for me." He nodded in the direction of the lift where a group of kids stood, watching them. "Maybe we could go for a walk later."

He glanced back at his friends, and she could tell he was anxious to go. *If I insist on talking now, they'll give him a hard time. I don't want to embarrass him.* "Sure. I mean about you needing to go. I understand." She didn't know what else to say.

In a flash, Hannah tried to formulate the many thoughts floating around her head into one succinct thought. *I can't go for a walk with you. We can't see each other anymore. I'm sorry. Thank you for the flowers, but I can't accept them.* Any of those would do.

"I can't walk," she blurted out.

Where did that come from? How come my mouth never gets the messages from my mind?

Brendan looked confused. "You seem to be doing okay right now," he said, glancing down at her feet.

"I mean . . . I can walk, just not with you."

"Can we have lunch today?"

"I can't do that."

"Coffee after lunch?"

She could tell he was getting frustrated.

"If it's in the lodge," she said.

"I'll meet you by the big fireplace at one." There was a note of impatience in his voice. "I need to go right now."

She didn't want him to go yet. "Thanks for the flowers," she blurted out.

His brow furrowed. "I didn't give you any flowers."

Hannah's mouth dropped open, but nothing came out.

He flashed another grin over his shoulder and skied toward the waiting group. "Maybe they were from Tyler," he called over his shoulder.

• • •

"I think they're from Brendan, but he won't admit it," Hannah told her friends.

Becca skied in perfect form, swishing back and forth through a small grove of pine trees. Jacie followed, and Hannah skied alongside on the outside of the grove in not-so-perfect form.

"Who else would give them to you?" asked Jacie.

Hannah shrugged her shoulders, throwing herself off balance and ending up on her rump. The snow was icier today, and she was falling more than yesterday. And today she didn't have anyone to help her up. She took out her camera to snap a couple of candid pics of her friends.

"Maybe you have a secret admirer," Becca said.

"Hey, wait up!" The girls looked up the mountain to see Solana's unmistakable jet-black hair flying out from under her bright ear warmers. She plowed to a stop beside them. She wasn't as new at skiing as Hannah, but she was far from being an expert like Becca.

"Where's Marcus?" asked Jacie.

"He's a jerk. Said he needed to do time trials with the team."

"Well, he *is* here with the ski team. You can't blame him for that," said Jacie.

"There are things that every man should know are more important than skiing. And I'm one."

As much as Hannah could be annoyed with Solana's arrogance, she also found herself fascinated by the confidence behind it.

Her own confidence lagged. What was she going to say to Brendan? And how? Did she really want to say anything? She remembered moments she had shared with Brendan. His smile, his laughter, *his touch*. And she wondered. Could she really pull off being Brendan's girlfriend? And even more—did she want to?

chapter 15

"You're sure you want to be alone with him again?" Jacie asked.

"We have to talk."

"Yeah . . . and who knows what else," Solana muttered under the roar of her blow-dryer. They had come in from the morning ski run and Solana didn't want to go down to lunch with her hair stringy. "Just be careful, *mi amiga*. Brendan isn't known for being a one-woman man."

The way he looks at me, I know there's no one else.

Hannah looked through her clothes and selected a long khaki skirt and a blue turtleneck sweater. She glanced in the mirror and noticed how well the sweater accentuated her eyes. *Would Brendan notice?* Hannah let her thoughts absorb her as she ran her brush through her long, blond hair.

She thought about his smile earlier that made her forget everything she had planned to say. He seemed to have that knack. Even the first time she'd met him, he had left her speechless.

If she looked at the situation rationally, she knew exactly what to do. But when she let herself think about *him*, her heart got everything confused. She closed her eyes so she could again feel his touch, the way he looked into her eyes, and the tender way he'd said her name. *And that kiss.*

"What are you smiling about?" Jacie asked, interrupting her private world.

"Smiling? I wasn't smiling," responded Hannah.

"Yes, you were," laughed Becca.

"And you still are," insisted Solana.

"No, I'm not." Hannah turned her back to the girls and pretended to busy herself putting clips into her hair. But she noticed in the mirror that the smile was still there.

Brendan wasn't the kind of boy she had hoped to marry . . . or was he? Her head and heart seemed to be in constant conflict. The only sure thing was that whenever he was within 10 feet, her heart won out.

● ● ●

Hannah sat by the fireplace inside the lodge leafing through a *Victorian Home* magazine that had been on the end table. She felt the weight shift on the leather couch and looked up to see Brendan, settling himself on the other side—a soft, confident smile on his lips.

"So, what did you want to talk about?" His deep brown eyes reflected the dancing flames. It reminded Hannah of Tyler's eyes last night. Brendan had the same strong jaw and intense look Tyler had. The comparison didn't last long as she became caught in Brendan's inviting look.

She had no doubt he knew she liked him. Hannah could see that pretty clearly. *I must cut things off now. But this will give me a chance to talk to him about what I'm thinking. It could be a wonderful witness to him if I explained why I feel the way I do about dating. What am I thinking? I can't do that. Here's my chance, right now. Brendan, I appreciate you, but I need to tell you that I can't see you. We should never have kissed. It was against my vow to wait until the day of my wedding . . .*

"Are you going to answer me or just continue looking coy and beautiful?" Brendan leaned closer. She looked deeply into his eyes—they seemed unending.

"You've got wonderful eyes," Hannah heard a voice that sounded like hers say.

"Thanks," Brendan said as he got up. "How about we head over to the coffee shop across the street. Is that okay?"

Hannah nodded. She wanted to stretch this moment to enjoy it as long as possible until she had to drop the big C-bomb. *Courtship*. What would he say? Would he go along with it? Would he say, "Whatever it takes to be near you?" But even if he agreed with courtship, they still couldn't be together right now. Her parents would never approve of that—she was too young. Or would he ask her to dismiss her family's ideals and date in secret?

He grabbed her hand as they crossed the street. His hand felt gentle and strong.

I might, she thought. *I might give up courtship if you ask me to.*

He held the glass door open for her and put his hand on the middle of her back to usher her through.

We could eat lunch together at school. The Brio gang would love him. He'd start coming out with us on Friday night at Becca's house, and then we'd all do things together on Saturday.

They stood in line at the shop. Brendan chattered on, excited about some runs he had been on that morning and some ideas he had for the newspaper. Hannah nodded with feigned interest because her mind was elsewhere.

He could join the youth group at church. We could go on retreats together and hang out at the Sunday night social. And we'd have the chance to be alone together sometimes. It wouldn't be too much, but just enough to have private conversations, and maybe share a few wonderful kisses.

The two sat across from each other. He with a double espresso cappuccino, she with hot chamomile tea. She hoped the chamomile would calm her nerves.

It won't be much longer—less than a year probably—before Mom and Dad will think I'm ready to be in a courting relationship. Brendan could talk to Dad. Dad would never have to know we'd already been seeing each other for a while. If he was going to our church it would seem like a natural choice to Mom and Dad. We'd have an intimate wedding ceremony. Would Sarah Ruth be okay with being flower girl? Or would she want to be a junior bridesmaid with Rebekah? If we explained it to her—

"So what was it you wanted to talk to me about?"

Here it goes.

"It's about us."

"What about us?"

"About my policies on dating."

Brendan raised his eyebrows over his coffee mug. "Your *policies?*"

"Well, actually, my family's policies." Seeing she had his full attention, she continued. "We believe in courtship, which means that before I date anyone, the guy has to talk to my dad first and my dad has to approve."

"Really?" he said. "That's . . . uh . . . interesting."

"And I also have to be at an age that my parents think I'm ready for marriage, because the whole point is that a couple spends time together with the intention of marriage. My family stays involved—kind of a way of protecting us."

"Okay."

"What I'm trying to say, Brendan," Hannah took a deep breath, "is that I shouldn't have kissed you when I did and I can't date you like you think we are." The words burst out, tumbling all over each other.

"What?"

She knew she was losing him, so she rushed on with the rest of her thoughts in one breath. "But we may have some other options. I'm thinking there are ways we could still hang out together—until my parents think I'm old enough to court. I just wouldn't tell my parents about it until then. I mean, you'd still have to meet them, but they wouldn't have to know how much we hang out. And then we can kind of keep dating like we are."

"I don't think we're dating." He seemed surprised.

"But we kissed!"

"I know. I remember." He laughed at her shocked response. "I just . . . Hannah . . ." He reached for her hand on the table, but she pulled it away. "I'm not the kind of guy who's tied to one girl. Ask anyone who knows me. I like playing the field."

Solana was right.

"I mean," he continued, probably realizing he had been insensitive, "I think you're a great girl and all. Really great."

Really great. I've heard that before.

"And the kiss was sweet . . ."

Sweet? I was planning my whole life around the passion of that kiss and he says it was "sweet."

"I only meant it as a sign of appreciation. You know, an I-had-a-nice-time-with-you-today kinda kiss."

I'd like to show you an I-had-a-nice-time-with-you-today kinda slug in the face. She was surprised by her own anger. She couldn't remember feeling this way before.

"I'm sorry if I gave you the wrong impression," he was saying. "I mean, we're very different people. I wouldn't expect to date you—ever."

Hannah smiled sweetly. "Of course. I'm just glad we got it all cleared up. I feel much better now."

● ● ●

"He should have called by now," Solana whined while she filed her long, manicured nails. "Marcus promised he'd call when he got back from his afternoon skiing."

"Maybe something came up," Jacie said. "We're supposed to meet the buses in 10 minutes; you'll probably see him down there."

"Ten minutes?" said Becca, looking at the clock. "I need to go pack." But she leaned back in her chair and continued flipping mindlessly through the channels.

"I'm done," said Solana, gesturing toward a mass of clothes overflowing out of an oversized duffel bag. She continued filing. "Y'know that new guy, Todd, seems pretty cute. I keep catching him staring at me, too. Marcus might miss out if he's not careful."

Hannah kept glancing toward the phone. Even after the disheartening talk she'd had with Brendan earlier, she still hoped he would call. There had been a spark—she knew it. How could he say it had only been a friendly kiss? Hadn't he felt the electricity? Didn't he get that falling feeling when they looked into each other's eyes? Even if he did call right now, they wouldn't have enough time to talk. She had no idea what she would say to him. Her mind spoke to her in a practical tone. "This clearly isn't the will of God, and my parents would never approve." But her heart screamed, "I've never felt more alive and more beautiful than when I'm with him." There had to be something more than Brendan would admit.

When their conversation ended, he had told her that he was meeting some guys to ski down the other side of the mountain. "Some last-minute-living-on-the-wild-side kinda stuff," he had said, then walked out.

She had watched him go, feeling as though she had put her heart on a platter in front of him, and he had ignored it. She couldn't bear the thought that she had tried to give him something that meant so much to her and so little to him. It was too painful to believe. *It had to mean more.*

Solana whined again, and Jacie answered her. "Maybe he's waiting for you downstairs, Solana, planning to share a seat with you on the way back."

Maybe . . . maybe Brendan's waiting for me downstairs, and he'll ask if we could ride back to Copper Ridge together. Then we could talk all the way home, just like we did on the way up. Hannah stopped short. Was that really only two days ago? So much had happened since then.

A knock on the door interrupted her thoughts. Hannah's heart leaped. *Brendan*. Of course, he had decided to come up here to help her carry her stuff down and then they would find a place to talk. *I knew he'd come through.*

Solana emerged from the bathroom armed with hotel-sized shampoos, conditioners, and lotions. "Someone else will have to get it."

Jacie barely got the door open when Megan burst inside.

"Hannah, ohmigosh, like, where have you been?"

"I've been right here," she said, irritated that it wasn't Brendan. Then she noticed Megan's pale face. "Megan? Are you okay? What's going on?"

"Yeah, I'm okay, but I just, like, swallowed my gum. But that doesn't matter because the worst thing that could possibly happen just did. Oh, Hannah, it's terrible."

"What? What is it?"

Solana, Becca, and Jacie stood and waited.

"It's Brendan."

"What about him?"

"He was in an accident. Hannah—" her voice broke "—he wasn't breathing."

chapter 16

A dark cloud of silent concern blanketed the bus on the way home—a stark contrast to the hurricane of laughter and chatter present on the previous trip. Everyone was thinking the same thing: *Would Brendan be okay? What would happen to him?*

Hannah continuously replayed the fragments of information Megan had told her. The group of guys were on the back side of the mountain, a section that had been roped off and deemed unsafe. Brendan took the lead over some jumps. A boulder shrouded with snow hid at the bottom of one jump. Brendan went first, 20 feet straight down to a churning thud of body on rock. The others found him unconscious, lying face up in crimson-colored snow. Marcus sat with Brendan while the others went for help. A helicopter was summoned to airlift them. No one knew anything else.

Please, God. Please let him be okay. Don't punish him because of me. She felt her fleeting prayer bounce off the ceiling of the bus and back into her lap. *What if Brendan died?* She still didn't know if he was a Christian. And here she had been so selfish, thinking about how he made her feel and how good it felt to be held and touched and liked. Why would God listen to *her?* She had disappointed Him again and again. He was probably shaking His head at her right now.

I didn't share Christ with Brendan. I'm a horrible witness to Solana and everyone else at school. I even doubted my parents' wisdom.

Hannah rested her forehead against the fogged windowpane and wiped a small spot clear so she could look outside. There wasn't much to see—only the dark of night interspersed with the occasional cluster of lights from small mountain villages.

As the bus neared Copper Ridge, the questions kept coming. *Is this my fault? Is it my failure that caused this to happen? What if Brendan dies? What if he goes to hell? It will be my fault. I should have told him about Jesus. I should have shared with him. I can share the gospel with clerks stacking melons at the grocery store, but I don't even mention it once during a three-hour bus ride or half a day skiing with someone I know.*

She let her forehead thud against the window. Somehow the pain made her feel a little better. What if God was getting rid of Brendan because he was a stumbling block to her? If she had been stronger with Brendan, maybe God wouldn't have allowed this to happen. But she hadn't been strong. And now God was punishing her—and Brendan.

Please, God. I promise if You let Brendan live, I'll find out if he's a Christian. And I'll share the gospel with him if he's not. And I won't kiss him until we're married. And I won't assume that we're going to get married. I promise, God. Just please help him. Don't let him die.

● ● ●

"How was the trip, honey?" Mrs. Connor's voice reached the entranceway before her welcoming face appeared. Hannah shut the door behind her and returned her mom's tight hug.

"Good," Hannah said, beginning the process of hanging up her coat and taking off her boots. *What can I say? I can't lie.* "I learned a lot about skiing." For her mom's benefit she ended the thought with what she hoped was a perky, carefree smile.

"What did Brendan think of your work?"

Brendan. What do I say about him? "He liked it, Mom. Too bad he's dying so he won't see the developed pictures." In the past, this was the sort of thing she would share with her mom in a second. She always told her mom everything. They would pray together about the hard stuff and Hannah would feel better. But for the first time Hannah could remember, she didn't want to say anything. She felt like she was drowning in guilt. She didn't want to have to tell her mom that she may be directly responsible for someone dying because she was a slut, and selfish, and a horrible witness.

Mrs. Connor must have noticed Hannah's dumbfounded expression. "That's the name of your editor, right? What did he think of how you did?"

"Oh, Brendan!" she said, as though she hadn't thought of him in days. "He seemed to think I did pretty well."

You did great. Really great. The tender words still echoed in her head. And so did the I-had-a-nice-time-today kinda kiss.

"Are you okay, sweetie?" Mrs. Connor knew her daughter too well. She searched Hannah's face for a clue.

Who is this awful person in my body? I lie to my parents; I'm a bad example to my younger siblings; I send people to hell.

For a brief moment, Hannah thought she could spill everything to her mother. Tell her how disappointed she was with herself, how God must hate her, and yet how she didn't even regret it sometimes. After all, she still thought about being near Brendan. His touch, the way the kiss felt. But would her mom ever be able to look at her the same again? After 16 years of guarding her purity, her perfect daughter was tarnished. She was supposed to be the role model, the godly example—and now look at her. She couldn't bear being a disappointment to her mother.

"I'm fine, Mom," Hannah said with as much assurance as she could muster. She grabbed her mom's hand for emphasis. "The weekend just took a lot out of me, especially with the pressure of my first assignment."

Mrs. Connor still didn't seem convinced. "You felt okay about how the shoots went, then?"

"They went better than I ever expected." *That, at least, is true.*

Her mom's face was still filled with concern. *She knows something is wrong. It's my mother—she loves me. Maybe I could tell her.* The house seemed pretty quiet, but she first wanted to make sure no one would interrupt them. "Where are Dad and Micah?"

Her mom nodded toward the den as they walked arm in arm into the living room. She could hear voices through the cracked door.

Mrs. Connor took a deep breath and shook her head. "Micah got himself in some trouble while you were gone."

Hannah could hear the rumblings of her dad's voice behind the den door.

"One of the ladies from church saw he and a girl cuddling together. Why don't you sit down and rest for a minute, Hannah. When we're done talking with Micah, I'll make us some tea." Hannah nodded and settled onto the couch.

Her mom slipped into the den, neglecting to close the door all the way.

"Are you ready to provide for this girl?" she heard her dad's angry voice question.

"I can take her out for a Coke, and that's all she wants right now. She's not asking me to help take care of babies." Hannah could imagine her father wincing at that statement.

"The point is, Micah, we had an agreement. And you outright disobeyed us." Mr. Connor's voice was stern and laced with tension.

"But I like this girl. I only wanted to spend time with her. Is that a crime?"

Mrs. Connor's voice broke in. "Of course it's not wrong to be her friend. But we feel you are too young to be spending that kind of time alone with a girl. We want you to learn to respect her."

"I *was* respecting her." Micah's words rose in anger. "She thought so, too."

"She might not understand right now—"

"She does understand," Micah interrupted. "She understands putting my arm around her isn't such a huge, awful, horrible thing."

Hannah gulped. *I sure can't talk to Mom about this now. What I did was a whole lot worse than that.* She felt sick to her stomach.

"Micah, you might think that what you did wasn't too bad," Hannah heard her mom's firm voice interpose. "There are probably going to be a lot of girls that you're going to like, and if you become emotionally attached to every one of them, not only do you harm yourself, but you'll be leaving a lot of hurt and confused young women behind. Think of Hannah."

"What about her?" Micah asked. Hannah held her breath in the other room. *Where was Mom going with this one?*

"You love your sister. And you should treat every young woman as a sister in Christ. Would you want a bunch of guys being flirtatious and physical with her?" Mom asked.

"Maybe it wouldn't be all that bad for Hannah to have some guy in her life. It might loosen her up," Micah said.

Mr. Connor had been quiet long enough. "Regardless of who needs to loosen up, you're going to need some reins for a while. You're grounded for the next two weeks."

"Two weeks?" Micah acted as though he'd been condemned to the salt mines.

"It's not only the fact that you were alone and being physically affectionate with a girl, but if I recall correctly, we had an agreement."

Micah sighed heavily.

"Which was—" his dad prompted.

"That I had to come home after youth group."

"When after youth group?"

"Right after." Micah's voice got softer and less combative.

"Did you obey?"

"No."

"Then is it reasonable for your parents to have consequences for that disobedience?"

"Yes, sir," Micah replied, defeated. "May I be excused now?"

"I'm not done yet. Over the course of these next two weeks, you will write an essay on the benefits and godliness of courtship. Do you understand the assignment?"

"Yes, sir."

"Then you may be excused."

Micah wasted no time. He was out of the den and through the back door with such speed, that he didn't even notice Hannah sitting on the couch. She saw him through the panes of the kitchen door, kicking at mounds of snow. She needed to talk to him. He would understand what she had done. He would understand how she felt.

She slipped out the door, wrapping her arms around her sweater to hold in the heat. He didn't look up.

"Micah." Her soft voice almost disappeared in the cool wind. "I couldn't help but hear—"

"You're just as bad as they are, Hannah," said Micah into the darkness, his back turned toward her.

"I know you're upset . . ." Suddenly the nerve drained out of her. She wanted to tell him she understood, she wanted to say she wondered about Mom and Dad's way of doing things, too, sometimes. She wanted to say that she'd messed up and she didn't know what to think about it. But nothing like that came out. Instead, terrifying concerns materialized. *What if I tell him the wrong thing? What if my questioning of Mom and Dad only gives him more fuel for his fire and he completely rebels—even ends up in prison? God would surely punish me for that.*

The 'good face' of Hannah emerged.

"I don't think you realize that it's for your own good. Someday you'll understand," Hannah said. She had never felt more like a hypocrite.

"Give me a break, Sis." He rarely called Hannah that anymore. "You're just as confused as I am." He turned to look at her, his eyes biting. "But at least I have the guts to think on my own."

He looked away again and trudged off. As soon as he escaped the porch light, she lost him in the moonless night.

And now I've driven my own brother away. Great, Hannah. Just great.

chapter 17

Hannah ascended the two flights of stairs to her attic bedroom. She loved her haven, and now she needed it more than ever. An afghan her grandmother had knitted for her when she was a baby lay across her bed, with a down comforter folded at the foot. All she wanted to do was crawl under the sheets and have a good cry.

Dropping her duffel bag to the floor, she noticed a letter on her bed addressed to her in familiar, perfect cursive. Aubrey. *If she knew what I had done—*

She could now add Aubrey to the list of people who would be disappointed with her; who would think of her as a horrible Christian. Of course, when God is upset with you, what does it matter if another person is let down? Hannah picked up the envelope and broke the seal with her thumbnail.

Dear Hannah,

I'm praying for you and hoping that life is getting better. I know it must be hard to leave good Christian friends and start over in a place where people have only lukewarm relationships with God. Perhaps He put you there for the purpose of being salt and light to a fallen generation. It may be through your steadfast suffering and dedication to purity that those who don't know Christ can see Him. We can only hope and pray. Stay strong, Hannah. Remember "We can do all things through Him who gives us strength." Phil. 3:14.

Love, your sister in Christ,
Aubrey

Hannah slipped the afghan off her bed, drew it around her shoulders, and settled herself into her wicker chair. She lit a candle on her bed stand and watched the flame flicker, casting dancing shadows across the room. Picking up Aubrey's letter again, she reread it. It sounded so much like what Hannah herself would have written a friend in the same situation—a friend who she thought truly was being strong and not just putting up a good front. But that wasn't her. She had failed—over and over again.

For the first time that she could remember, Christianity didn't seem that simple. It seemed impossible. *How could I ever be that good? How can I keep it up? I've tried my whole life to be this godly person, and now I've ruined it all in one weekend.*

At the same time she felt herself resenting Aubrey. Was it because she was jealous that Aubrey was better than she? That things were simpler for her? The letter felt heavy—the weighty expectations it represented were too much to handle. She refolded the flowered piece of stationery and returned it to the envelope. Then, without even thinking about it, she allowed the corner of it to catch the frolicking flame. The orange glow made its way up the edge of the envelope, slowly consuming the precise handwriting etched on the envelope and the "holy" words inside.

• • •

Hannah bustled into school Monday morning. It wasn't an accident that she arrived uncharacteristically late. Well, late for her at least, which meant right before the first bell. Just enough time to make it to class without being marked tardy. *Anything to avoid running into someone from the ski trip*. She still didn't know how Brendan was doing, and she had been praying nonstop for his recovery.

"Hannah!" a voice called. Hannah spun around. It was Kelli.

Hannah forced a smile. "Hi!"

Kelli didn't even pretend. Her narrowed eyes spoke loud and clear, but the words were even sharper. "I don't get you. Who are you really?"

Hannah stopped dead in her tracks, oblivious to the rush of students swarming around them. "What do you mean?"

"You say all the right things and, I admit, it sounds pretty good. But you're such a . . . a hypocrite." Kelli practically spat the accusation at her.

Hannah felt queasy in the pit of her stomach. Kelli must have heard—somehow—about what happened between her and Brendan. Maybe even with Tyler. And here she was trying to persuade Kelli to choose courtship for her life, and this is the example she gave? Others probably knew then, too. Would the whole school be laughing and pointing and whispering about her now?

Hannah steered Kelli into an alcove between two classrooms. "I'm really sorry," she said, her words pouring out of her like a waterfall. "I feel awful about it. I know it was wrong."

"Yeah, it was." Kelli's fury seemed to have lessened a little, but she was still clearly upset. "I just don't understand what made you think you could do such a thing!"

"How did you find out, anyway?" Hannah asked. She didn't want to turn the conversation to her own concerns, but she was dying to know how it got out and how many other people were aware of it. For all she knew, it would be on the front page of the newspaper next week. Hannah envisioned two shots—one of her and Tyler, the other of her and Brendan—side by side. The caption would read in big, bold letters:

REBEL COURTSHIP GIRL GOES EXTREME

"My dad told me. He wasn't very happy."

"Your dad?" How in the world did Mr. Hendricks find out? This was too bizarre. And after she had written him that letter, too. Now he'd never listen. "I don't know what I was thinking, and I don't know how to fix it because now everyone knows I'm kissing everyone, and I know your dad must be upset, but if you'll—if he'll—just give me the chance to explain—"

"Wait a second," Kelly interrupted. "You're kissing everyone?"

"Is that what he said?" Hannah couldn't believe how fast rumors spread and how distorted they became. "Not everyone. Just Brendan and Tyler."

"You kissed Brendan and Tyler? Wow. We need to talk." Kelli looked incredulous, but there was a small smile on her face.

"You didn't know? I thought you said your dad told you."

"No," Kelli said, laughing. "My dad doesn't keep up with all the high school gossip. He told me about the letter you sent him."

"Oh."

"He didn't appreciate you telling him how to raise his daughter. It was pretty embarrassing. And after all that you had said about honoring our parents, I thought it was pretty disrespectful."

"Oh. I see. I'm sorry."

The halls were almost empty. "We really need to get to class, but I do want to talk to you about something later."

"Okay."

"And, Hannah," she said running the opposite way down the hall. "I'm kind of glad you're not perfect."

•••

Hannah's mind wandered during her third-period psychology class. While Mr. Faulkner discussed tomorrow's assignment, she was replaying moments with Brendan, the kiss with Tyler, and her conversation with Kelli. She wondered how Brendan was doing and how her mistake would affect Kelli's walk with the Lord. An all-class groan brought her back to the present.

"It's one page, ladies and gentlemen," Mr. Faulkner said in response to the class reaction. "Title it: *My Greatest Fear*."

Hannah started to retrieve her planner so she could write the assignment down and noticed, amid the daydreaming, she had been mindlessly doodling on her returned quiz. *Brendan. Brendan Curtis. Mrs. Brendan Curtis. Hannah Curtis.* She quickly began to erase the names, hoping no one else had seen them. *Tyler.* His name was written boldly in the middle of the page.

•••

"Did you ever figure out who gave you the flowers?" Tyler asked at lunch that day.

"No. And at this point, I don't care." It was true. Any curiosity she may have normally felt was shadowed by the stress and confusion of the last couple days.

"I think it's romantic," said Jacie. "A secret admirer. It could be anyone."

"Yeah, and we all know Hannah needs more men in her life. She has a whole selection of love-struck puppies." Solana said it under her breath, but both Tyler and Hannah turned a little red.

Hannah quickly switched the subject. "So is everyone done with their Christmas shopping? It's only a little over two weeks away."

The rest of the group shook their heads.

"Done with it? I haven't even started," said Tyler.

"I've gotten a couple gifts. Are you done, Hannah?" asked Jacie.

"I usually try to finish up by the end of October." She was embarrassed to say it. Another bit of evidence that Hannah Connor was the odd one out.

Hannah excused herself soon after, saying she needed to go to the newspaper office. She hadn't mentioned anything about Brendan except that she was still praying for him. And that was only after Jacie asked if she had heard any news. But, in truth, her concern for him incessantly nagged at her.

"Megan," she said, recognizing the frizzy red hair without the girl needing to turn around. "Have you heard about Brendan? Is he okay?"

"Like, yeah! You haven't heard?" she asked, her mouth dropping open, exposing her fruit-flavored gum. Then her tone shifted. "Come to think of it, though, I just, like, found out about two or three minutes ago, so I'm not really, like, surprised."

"So what's the news?"

"Oh, he's, like, fine. Well, fine for someone who's in the hospital hooked up to a bunch of machines."

Hannah pictured Brendan in an indefinite coma, his family standing vigil over him trying to decide whether or not they should pull the plug. "What kind of machines? Is he on life support?"

"Actually, maybe he's not on machines. I just, like, think of that when someone is in the hospital. He's beaten up, like, a broken leg and . . . uh . . ." she paused thoughtfully. Hannah could tell Megan had no idea what she was talking about. "And some other broken things. But he's conscious. His mom said he could even have, like, visitors. Some of us are going after school. Like, do you want to come?"

"Maybe." Hannah didn't know what she should do, but she knew she didn't want to talk to Brendan with a bunch of other people around.

"Like, okay. We're meeting in the art room, like, right after school to make a banner and stuff. You can, like, meet us there if you want." Her gum snapped. "We'll carpool. Do you, like, have a car?"

Hannah nodded. "I have my parents' car today." *Maybe I can get over there before everyone else. We could talk for a few minutes alone. If I leave right after the bell . . .*

"That's so cool. I always told my parents I wanted, like, a red convertible. I love convertibles. Then for, like, Christmas they get me this, like, red Matchbox convertible, and they think it's, like, all a funny joke. And I'm, like, well, that's lame. You get a laugh, and I *still* don't get a car . . ."

Megan trailed on, but Hannah wasn't listening. She had to think about what she was going to say to Brendan. She had to set the record straight. *Thanks, God*, she prayed silently. Brendan was getting another chance. And she was going to keep her promise to God.

● ● ●

Hannah checked the room number once more. 1447—that's it.

What do I say? What do I do? Go in there and give him a big smack on the lips? No . . . no . . . no. Although I can imagine his surprise. No, I'll say hello and ask him how he's doing. But with deep concern in my voice. She flashbacked to nursing home visits with the church, the leaders emphasizing that visitors should come across as happy, not worried. *Maybe something breezy and lighthearted. Yeah.*

She tapped her knuckles on the door, not wanting to disturb him if he was sleeping.

"Come in," called the voice from inside.

Hannah swallowed and put on her cheeriest smile. Her palms were sweating as she clutched the bouquet of bright yellow daisies. "Hi! How are you?" she said, coming in the door. *Breezy—that was definitely breezy*, she thought.

"Hi, Hannah!" Brendan put down the book he was reading and flashed her his most welcoming grin.

"How are you doing?" Hannah made a mental note that he was

reading instead of watching television. It showed a constructive use of time.

"Despite a broken leg and a couple broken ribs, a few stitches in the old noggin'—" he touched the bandage on his head and winced. "Really. I've never been better." He winked. Even cooped up in a hospital bed and hooked up to an IV, Brendan still seemed the picture of vigor and health.

"I brought these for you," she said, thrusting the happy bouquet in front of his face. *And hopefully you're not allergic to them since I just pretty much stuffed them up your nose*, she added to herself.

"Thanks," he said.

"Can I get you anything? A glass of water? Another pillow?" She noticed he seemed a little uncomfortable.

"Naw, I'm good."

"Are they taking pretty good care of you?"

"Too good." He grinned at her, causing her to grin back. "This one nurse, Brumhilda, has made it her life's calling to poke, prod, and check my vitals as much as possible. She's so strict and regulated about it, I feel like I should salute her every time she comes in the room."

"Well, at least she's watching out for you."

"True. Although it *will* be nice to be able to go to the bathroom by myself again."

"Well, you know I'll be happy to help in any way I can." As soon as the words came out of her mouth, she realized how that must have sounded. Red-faced, she began back-peddling. "I mean . . . I meant . . . not with that, of course, I'm sure you'll be great at that. I mean, doing it by yourself. I was thinking like helping you—y'know, carry books, get around . . . but not to the men's room, of course—"

Brendan couldn't stifle his laughter any longer. "Hannah, you better stop before you dig yourself too deep into that pit." He paused. "I'm really glad you're here. You're better than ibuprofen at helping me feel better."

Hannah's heart did a little dance. *Did he really mean that?*

She pushed away the thoughts—she couldn't lose track of the reason she was there. *I guess this is as good a time as any*. "I'm always encouraged when God answers prayers, aren't you?" she asked, trying to sound casual.

Brendan's expression had "Huh?" written all over it.

"I mean, I've been praying for your recovery, and you're doing so well. It *must* be a miracle of God."

Brendan straightened his shoulders and gave a cocky half smile. "My doctors attributed it to a quick rescue and the fact that I keep myself in good shape. But since you prayed, I can give God a little credit, too," he added as though he were being generous.

Hannah dug through her purse for her spiral-bound prayer notebook. "See," she explained, flipping open the black-and-white cover, "I write down all sorts of requests, and then I pray for them—every day. And once they're answered, I check them off." She pointed his name out to him and made a bold check mark by it with a felt-tipped pen, as though that would prove to him beyond a doubt that this was, indeed, the hand of God.

"Thanks, Hannah." His gratitude struck her as condescending.

"It says in the Bible—in Philippians 4:6—that 'with prayer and thanksgiving let your requests be made known to God.' "

"Yeah, I've heard that, too."

"You have?"

"Of course. I told you I go to church."

"But do you believe it?" The words stuck in her throat like peanut butter.

"Well, sure . . . I guess." He shifted nervously in his bed.

"Because going to church doesn't mean you're going to heaven. You need to have a personal relationship with Christ for that."

"I know, Hannah."

"You do?"

"I said my prayer of salvation in Bible school probably 10 years ago."

"That's wonderful!" Hannah clapped her hands together once, unable to contain her excitement. *Thank you, God.*

"Yeah. It's a hoot."

Pause. *Uh-oh.*

"Were you sincere?" she asked.

Brendan paused, staring past her to the door. He looked like he wanted to make a run for it. "Sure. It's just not as important to me as it is to you. I mean, I think religion and all that is fine, but it doesn't fit my style right now." His eyes met hers again. "No offense, but I don't want to spend my life sitting around hospitals showing everyone my prayer book."

"Well, I go other places, too," Hannah said, her voice rising in defense.

"It's just that I'm 17—you know what I mean? I have a lot of living I want to do."

"But what if it's not as much as you think? Brendan, you could have died out there this past weekend—"

"But I didn't."

"By the grace of God."

"Or by modern medical technology."

Stalemate.

The door opened and in came the nurse Hannah knew must be "Brumhilda." A large and domineering woman, she reminded Hannah of a cross between a cafeteria lady and the sergeant in the *Beetle Bailey* comic strip.

"Time to change the IV bag," she commanded. Hannah looked around, almost convinced that the nurse was telling her to do it.

"Brendan!" A sea of teenagers suddenly flooded through the open door behind her. Brumhilda vainly attempted to stifle the chaos by putting her finger to her lips and repetitively shushing, but the dozen or so teens didn't even notice. They were too anxious to see what Brendan thought of the large “Get Well Soon!” banner they were toting in behind them.

“How ya doin’, man?”

“You had us so scared!”

“Hey . . . nice cast. Talk about a fashion statement!”

“Look at that head bandage.”

“You look like Frankenstein with those stitches. How many’d ya get?”

Caught in the swarm of well-wishers, Hannah was inadvertently pushed aside. She watched Brendan’s animated expressions as he fielded the hundred questions and conversations, all the while trying to calm the plum-faced Brumhilda. Hannah knew her discussion with Brendan was over, and she glanced around trying to find a familiar face. No one. Except Megan, and she was busy balancing herself on two stacked chairs hanging the banner.

“Excuse me, please.” Hannah stuck her face in between two girls at Brendan’s side and interrupted his somewhat exaggerated version of the accident. “I need to go, Brendan. Hope you’re back at school soon.”

“Thanks for coming by,” he said offhandedly before resuming his story.

She stepped out into the hall, which seemed dead quiet compared to Brendan’s busy room. Her footsteps echoed in the hall. It seemed appropriate somehow—she felt very alone.

chapter 18

Hannah Connor
Psychology I

My Greatest Fear

My greatest fear is that I'll be alone for the rest of my life. In committing myself to courtship, I've agreed to give up my own attempts to find a marriage partner and have put this decision in the hands of God and my parents. It is my belief that if God wants me to be married, He will bring that person into my life.

But what if God doesn't come through in finding me someone to marry? What if I follow courtship to the letter and my future husband never enters the picture? What if I end up living in a little apartment all by myself with nine cats and countless knitting projects, watching game shows on television for 12 hours a day and devouring frozen pizzas? And then when my teeth fall out, I'll survive on banana milkshakes. There I would be: 400 pounds, a pile of cat fur on my lap, watching Vanna White's granddaughter turn letters.

Hannah ripped the page out of her notebook and tore it to shreds. *How faithless of me to not trust God with this.* She knew she couldn't hand it in even if it was true. What if her psychology teacher wasn't a Christian? What kind of witness would that be for Christ?

Hannah Connor
Psychology I

My Greatest Fear

My greatest fear is that I'll do something that will make God *really mad at me and He'll decide that He doesn't love me anymore. Or, even if He does still love me, He'll punish me—turn His back on me. Which I probably deserve. Why should He still protect me or make my life go well after what I did?*

Hannah sighed, her eyes nearly overflowing with tears. As she tore up her second draft she realized her greatest fear might be coming true.

Silence reigned at dinner that evening. Micah and Mr. Connor were still irritated with each other from the night before. Hannah had sunk into her own thoughts and didn't make any effort to lighten things up. The rest of the family could only attempt to maintain the peace.

"Would you please pass the salt?" Mrs. Connor requested.

Suddenly the front door slammed shut, jolting Hannah from her thoughts.

"Hey, where is everyone?"

The perky, pseudoangry call came from the front entranceway. And the entire family immediately knew who it was.

"Just once it would be nice if she called before she stopped by," Hannah's dad mumbled to himself. But he smiled widely and jumped from the table as the rest of the family stampeded past him in their hurry to get to the front door. "But that wouldn't be Dinah," he said as he dropped his napkin next to his plate and joined the mob eager to greet her.

By the time Hannah reached the scene, it was already a mass of hugs, kisses, laughter, and luggage.

Aunt Dinah handled it all with her sparkling smile and easy laugh. She knelt down to hug each of the children individually. As Dinah spoke with Rebekah, Elijah tried to climb onto her back and Sarah Ruth clung tightly to her arm. Micah hung up Aunt Dinah's leather jacket and Mom commented on Dinah's new hairstyle. She had gone short this time—almost pixieish. It matched her slight, 5'2" build and fairylike face perfectly.

Dinah caught sight of Hannah and stood to hug her. Aunt Dinah had the best hugs—long, tight, and warm. It was the kind of hug that made someone know this was a hug that meant something, not just a polite formality.

"Oh, Hannah. It's so good to see you." She released her arms and looked Hannah directly in the eyes. "*You* are beautiful."

"Thanks." It was a compliment only Aunt Dinah could get away with. When her friends told her she was attractive, it made her self-conscious. But when Aunt Dinah said it, Hannah simply believed it. *I believed it when Brendan said it, too.*

"I'm going to be here for a few days," she said, never breaking eye contact. "We'll need to get together for a woman-to-woman chat sometime, 'kay?" She scooped Sarah Ruth into her arms and hung the laughing child upside down.

"I'd love to." Hannah laughed at Sarah Ruth's delighted squeals.

"So look who the cat dragged in," her father's voice boomed out. "Doesn't a brother get any attention?"

Aunt Dinah gave Hannah a wink before hugging her big brother. "Hey, Teddy-boy. I saved the best for last."

"You'd better believe it," he teased, squeezing his little sister with great affection. "What brings you here?" he asked, his arm still around her while he moved her toward the sofa.

"Oh, the usual—business. But I couldn't go right through Colorado without seeing my favorite family, could I?"

Dinah stopped by when she had the chance, but it was always spontaneous. They never knew when to expect her or how long she would stay. But while she was there, she would entertain them with a never-ending abundance of exciting stories. Last time she visited she shared with them her experience of bungee-jumping off Victoria Falls and getting invited to the prime minister's house in England, after accidentally running into him on her bike. She had everyone laughing to tears.

Rebekah was making herself comfortable on the living room couch and patting the sofa cushion next to her. "Aunt Dinah, come sit next to me. Tell us a story!"

Dinah laughed. "First, how about some gifts?" None of the children argued with that, and she handed out beautifully carved wooden animals from Costa Rica.

Gretchen Connor took Dinah's hand as she received the gift. "Dinah, that's a beautiful ring," she said, a curious look on her face.

"Yes, isn't it nice?" Dinah smiled, her eyes dancing.

"Did you get it in Costa Rica?" asked Sarah Ruth, tearing her eyes away from her carved giraffe to look.

"Nope."

"Iceland?" suggested Daniel. He had a thing about Iceland.

"Try again."

"It looks European to me," said Micah, taking hold of his aunt's hand to look at it.

"Not quite. Try Denver."

"Sounds exotic," smiled Hannah. "When were you there?" The state capital was only an hour away.

"Just this past weekend. Visiting a friend." Dinah looked uncharacteristically self-conscious. She looked at the ring, and a huge smile crossed her face. She looked up, her eyes moist. "I'm engaged!"

Hannah thought she heard her dad's jaw hit the floor. Her mom's eyes were as big as pancakes. The children went crazy, tackling and hugging Aunt Dinah. Hannah added herself to the haphazard pile.

"Who is this man, Dinah?" Mr. Connor asked, brotherly concern in his voice.

Dinah sat upright and straightened her disheveled clothes. She spoke in that dreamy sort of way that assured Hannah that her aunt was very much smitten. "His name is Michael. He's an assistant pastor at a church in Denver. We've been good friends for years, but a few months ago we ran into each other in Germany. He was leading a missions group and I kind of joined in to help out. And the rest," she flung her arms out, "is history."

"Why haven't you said anything about him before? Why haven't we met him?" Mr. Connor's eyes narrowed. "I want to meet him before you finalize this idea."

"Teddy-boy, trust me. He's wonderful. I didn't want to say anything until I knew for sure. You'll meet him soon. It's a good thing. Very good."

"A *pastor?*" Mom's question came out more like a squeak. Hannah knew what her mom must be thinking, because Hannah was thinking the same thing. If Aunt Dinah was going to get married, it would be to an archaeologist or a skydiving instructor. A pastor seemed too, well, *normal*.

"How will you settle down, Dinah?" asked Mr. Connor. "You're busy flying around the world trying to kill yourself. You won't even have time to get married."

Dinah laughed at his teasing. Then she became as serious as Hannah had ever seen her. "I'm almost 30 years old, Ted. I'm ready for this. I've never wanted to settle down before, but being with Michael makes me want a marriage, a house, a family."

"A family?" Another squeak from Mom.

"Yeah, y'know, one of those two-parents-and-a-bunch-of-kids kind of arrangements." She wrapped her arms around the Connor children and cocked her head with a smile. "You may have heard of it."

Mrs. Connor wiped her eyes and hugged Dinah. "I'm so happy for you."

"Me, too," Mr. Connor said. "If I can get over the shock."

As Hannah walked the Stony Brook halls the next day, there seemed to be 10 times the number of couples there had been last week. Guys with an arm slung over a girl's shoulder. Close, head-to-head conversations by the lockers. She watched a couple stroll down the hall, his fingers intertwined with hers. He stopped her, sliding his arm behind her and pulling her close. She looked up at him and smiled, and they both started to laugh at some private joke. He tucked a stray lock of hair behind her ear and gave her a gentle kiss on the forehead. The girl pointed her eyes in Hannah's direction, and Hannah realized she was staring. She averted her eyes and kept walking.

But the picture stayed with her. It would be so nice to have someone like that in her life. Someone who she could share private jokes with, someone she could talk with about her good days and her bad days, someone who would always be waiting as she got out of class.

What is so wrong about wanting—or even having*—a boyfriend?*

At lunch, Hannah noticed Kelli coming out of the cafeteria. She debated whether to avoid her or catch up with her. On one hand, she was too embarrassed and ashamed to talk to Kelli. How could she convince Kelli of courtship when she didn't even know if she believed in it herself? And why would Kelli listen to her? On the other hand, she felt like she was a terrible witness and wanted to set the record straight.

Before she could decide, Kelli called out to her. Hannah took a deep breath and maneuvered her way across the busy hall.

"Hi! I'm glad I ran into you. I brought a book that you can give your dad to read," Hannah said, putting down her backpack and rummaging through it.

"Hannah, I told you, I decided not to do courtship."

"But what about what you said—"

"I've given it a lot of thought," said Kelli. "I think you have some good ideas, like having high standards for the guys I go out with and setting physical limits, but I don't need courtship in order to do those things."

"So you're still going to date like you used to?" Hannah stopped and looked at Kelli.

"Yes, I'm going to date. But not like I used to. If there's a good, Christian guy who asks me to the youth group ice-skating party, I'll go with him."

"Why can't you go with girlfriends and he can go with guy friends? Then you can observe his character in a group setting." Hannah could hear the urgency in her own voice. She didn't know why it was so important for her to convince Kelli. Maybe she thought that if she could persuade one person to change to a courtship lifestyle, God would forget about her own mistakes.

"Because I want to be able to have a one-on-one conversation with him if we decide to go out for coffee afterward. And I want to see how he would treat me as a date."

"You'd go out for coffee? Just the two of you? You're asking for trouble."

"I've decided on my boundaries—both emotional and physical. I've even written them out. Stuff like not being alone with a guy unless we're in a public place and making sure I know him pretty well before I go on a date with him. I don't think it's wrong to go out and have fun with a solid, Christian guy."

"You could still get hurt, Kelli. You could still kiss someone—even if you don't intend to. Sometimes your emotions get the best of you." A flash video of Brendan's mouth moving closer to hers invaded her thoughts.

"But sometimes a kiss is just a kiss. I mean, isn't the point of courtship to protect your heart, not your lips?"

Hannah was exasperated. "But the way we remain pure—"

"The way *you* remain pure, you mean."

"Well, it's the *right* way!"

"So you're saying that even if I loved God and committed my life to serving Him, but still dated guys who are strong Christians, I would be out of God's will."

"Yes," Hannah insisted. This was all going so fast that she didn't know if she really believed it or not.

"That doesn't make sense. If it's that important to God then why didn't He put a 'Thou shalt not hang around members of the opposite sex unless you're married to them' clause in the Ten Commandments?" Now Kelli's voice was rising, not in volume, but in pitch.

Hannah felt like a wave knocked her over. *Last week I would've been able to explain to Kelli why she is wrong. I would've known what to say. But now, I'm questioning everything that I ever believed about it myself. So how can I convince anyone else?*

"You're opening yourself up to a world of hurt," was all she could think to say. And she wondered if the words referred more to her own heart than to Kelli's situation.

"So are there any good guys out there?" asked Kelli.

"I wouldn't trust any of them." *Or at least not myself with them.*

"Not even your own brother?"

She thought of his latest actions. "Well, I don't know about Micah. He's done some questionable things. But it's not like I would date my brother, anyway."

"But what about *me* dating your brother?"

"You? But you don't even know him."

Kelli cocked her head, giving Hannah a funny look. "Of course I know him."

"You would want to date him?"

"Absolutely. He's a very sweet guy, Hannah."

And then it sank in. Flashbacks of the discussion between Micah and her parents. The tentative, knowing smile on the girl's face in front of her. The soft-spoken voice on the phone calling for him. "*You're* the one?"

Kelli nodded.

The big sister in her wanted to say, "Awww . . ." But the courtship part of her wanted to be upset with Kelli for causing all these problems in her family, for hurting her parents, for hurting *her*.

Hannah stared at Kelli. Since overhearing that conversation in the den, Hannah had pictured an obnoxious, overly hormonal, overly made-up, immature teenager, who was cute and flirty enough to somehow catch her brother's eye. But she could only describe the girl in front of her as sweet, loving, intelligent, and very mature. She didn't know what to think. It had been easier to dismiss Micah's "girlfriend" when she didn't have the face in front of her. And she had pictured Kelli with this jerk of a guy who was only trying to take advantage of her. But her brother was wonderful. Despite his attitude around the house, he truly respected others and was always a gentleman with women. On numerous occasions, Hannah had overheard freshmen girls talk about the latest chivalrous acts of Micah Connor.

Hannah didn't know what to think. In her heart she wasn't sure about courtship, but in her head, she was afraid not to be.

chapter 19

Hannah took Aunt Dinah to Copperchino. She thought her aunt would appreciate the unique atmosphere.

"I love it," Dinah said, sinking into the overstuffed couch. "Very fun."

"It's a great place to hang out. We come here a lot."

"The guy behind the counter doesn't mind, does he?" Aunt Dinah had a laugh in her voice.

"What do you mean?"

"Don't tell me you didn't realize he's interested in you."

"That's ridiculous. He doesn't even know me."

"He knows enough. You said you come in here pretty often."

"But I've never even had a conversation with him, besides 'One hot tea, please.' "

"Okay . . . how many times has he asked if we wanted our drinks heated up?" Dinah had a smirk on her face.

"A few. But the Copperchino always has good service."

"For you maybe. We've been here five minutes and he's asked us twice. Besides, he keeps looking at you."

Hannah looked up. Sure enough, the guy was watching her as he wiped down the front counter. He quickly averted his eyes.

"Again?" Hannah shook her head. "The girls said he was looking at me *last* time I was in here."

"Yes, it certainly seems this isn't the first time he's admired you from afar."

"I think he's in my English class. He's probably looking over here because he's heard what a freak I am," Hannah said.

"Maybe he's a nice guy. Maybe he just wants to talk to you." There was a glimmer of teasing on her face.

Hannah glared at her aunt. "I don't want to talk about him."

"Okay, okay, I'll lay off." Aunt Dinah set down her latte, her smile fading. She reached over and touched Hannah's arm. "But I do want you to tell me what's going on in your life."

"Well," Hannah leaned back on the couch and looked up toward the ceiling. "School is going okay. My grades are pretty good. Things at church are about the same as—"

"You know what I mean, Hannah Connor," Aunt Dinah interrupted. "What is going on with *you?* It's obvious something's been on your mind."

That's all the invitation Hannah needed to spill the whole story. Once she told about meeting Brendan and his impact on her, the subsequent events flowed freely. From the lift ride up to the ski ride down, from the kisses to the roses, from the accident to the hospital visit, and finally, to her conversation with Kelli that morning.

After she had poured out her heart, she paused, staring at her hands clenched in her lap. "I've messed up everything. Everything! No one else is going to try courtship now, and I'm not even sure if that's what I want to be doing. How can I so easily walk away from what I've always known to be right? God must hate me." Hannah wiped the tears dripping down her face.

Aunt Dinah sat silently for a minute.

She must be disappointed in me, too, Hannah thought.

Dinah finally spoke. "Do you have any idea how much I've messed up?"

"I know you got into a little trouble in high school, but Mom and Dad never went into details. What did you do? Get bad grades? Skip school?"

"Yeah." Dinah put her latte on the coffee table. "And partied."

Hannah looked at her, her eyes wide. "You *drank*?" Hannah didn't know what to think. Her beloved aunt drinking alcohol? Hannah took a sip of her vanilla steamer.

Dinah looked Hannah full into her eyes. "And got pregnant."

Hannah began choking on the hot drink. "Pregnant?" she asked between coughs. Her stomach lurched. Suddenly, drinking alcohol was nothing. *Not you, Aunt Dinah*, Hannah's heart pleaded. *Please tell me you're joking. Please tell me it's not true.*

"I started sleeping with my boyfriend because I thought I had to earn his love. He was very popular and I was only kind of popular. I thought we were being safe, but . . ." Her voice faded out into the obvious.

"What did you do?" Hannah asked, her voice barely a whisper.

"I decided to give her up for adoption. I was only 16." Dinah looked wistfully out the window. "I know it was the right decision. But you can't have something like that happen and not have it impact the rest of your life."

Hannah stared at her, stunned. Dinah waited.

Hannah wanted to say something. But what could she say? *How can I look up to Aunt Dinah ever again?*

Aunt Dinah continued. "Your dad was so helpful. I don't know what I would have done without him."

"Really?" Hannah remembered the times her father had expressed frustration at how quickly dating teenagers got physically close to each other. "I'd have thought he'd be furious with you."

Dinah chuckled. "Well, he was disappointed in the beginning. Your father has strong convictions based on Scripture, but he also knows how to help someone pick up and move forward. After all, you can't take back being pregnant."

"I still can't believe it." Hannah couldn't keep track of all this startling information. She thought her mind or her heart might explode from trying to make sense of it all.

"Your dad and mom were my strongest support. I had planned on having an abortion. But your parents took me in, saying they just wanted to talk with me and provide a place for me to think about my decision for a week. You were two at the time and Micah was a newborn. After that week of seeing a precious new life and playing with you, I knew I couldn't go through with an abortion." Dinah leaned over with tears in her eyes and hugged Hannah.

Hannah had no words. Even her mind was blank.

Dinah sat back and sipped her latte, patiently waiting, a hint of nervousness crossing her face. "So what do you think of your aunt now? Am I still your favorite?"

Hannah had never imagined that her aunt was capable of something like that. She set her steamer down. "I don't know what to say."

Dinah's voice grew soft. "I know. I'm sorry for asking that. It wasn't fair."

"I don't understand how you could have . . . how you would have . . ."

"When we take our eyes off God, we can make all kinds of stupid decisions. We let desire for something else rule our hearts and allow that to take us past what we know is right."

"That's what I did," Hannah said softly. "I can't believe I liked it," she said, feeling ashamed.

"You liked the kiss?"

"Shhh. Don't say it so loud." Hannah lowered her voice.

Dinah matched her volume. "Sorry. So . . . did you?"

"Yes. And worse, I'm still attracted to the boys—both of them!"

"That's wonderful."

"That's awful!"

Dinah laughed and pulled Hannah into a one-armed hug. "Congratulations! You are truly a red-blooded 16-year-old created and designed by the hand of God."

"Really?"

"Yes," Dinah said, reaching over to pat Hannah's hand. "What you felt is not only normal, but God-given. Hannah, I don't think what you did was so awful—"

"But it was *wrong*," Hannah said.

"That's a decision between you, God, and your parents. You have to figure out the best way to guard your heart."

"But what if we make the wrong decision?" Hannah bit her lip. She only wanted to please God, but she didn't know what that looked like right now.

"I think you'll be okay. You and your parents trust God for wisdom and you'll obey that answer when it comes."

Dinah turned Hannah's face toward her own. "You're a bright girl with a good heart. And you have parents who only want what's best for you. They're willing to sacrifice so much for what they believe is the best for all their children. After all, your talented mother, who could be making a good salary at a high-powered job, didn't bat an eye when she and your dad decided to homeschool. I tried to talk her out of it. But they made the right decision. You all have turned out to be the best six kids on the planet."

"You have to say that. You're our aunt," Hannah accused.

Dinah pretended to pout. "Maybe, but it's true." She reached out and took Hannah's hands in hers. "The ultimate truth we all have to learn is to let God be the one who satisfies our hearts, not finding temporary satisfaction in kissing every boy who comes along."

Hannah blushed. "I didn't kiss every boy."

"I know, I know. They kissed you." Dinah laughed and then became serious. "Hannah, I'm not one of those who feels it's wrong to have a kiss with someone you love before you're married. However, God calls different people to different ways of living. For you, if God has called you to save even your kisses for marriage, then there is forgiveness if you make a mistake. None of us is without sin. None of us is without need for forgiveness."

"*Did* you feel forgiven?" Hannah asked. "*Do* you feel forgiven?"

"Most of the time. That's why I shared my sordid story with you. To show you how His love doesn't end with our mistakes. His forgiveness is deeper than our worst sin. Your parents helped with that. The rest of the holy Connors 'washed their hands of me,' giving up on this heathen. But your parents loved me and accepted me in spite of my sin. They knew I was repentant. That's why I'm closest to your family." She paused. "And I praise God that He's more forgiving than some of His people."

Hannah's silence revealed that she was still reeling from what felt like an emotional punch in the stomach.

"Hannah—what do you think? Do my mistakes change who I am now?"

Hannah thought a moment. "I suppose that those mistakes are part of what made you who you are now."

"YES!" Aunt Dinah said. "Oh, I wish I hadn't done them. But thank God He can still do incredible things in my life despite my wrong choices."

Hannah considered that. Dinah was right. God *was* doing incredible things in Dinah's life. Her job took her all over the world. And every place she went, she showed God's love to others.

"Do you think God allows me to serve Him despite those wrong choices?"

"Absolutely."

Aunt Dinah focused on Hannah's eyes. "So can God forgive you for breaking your promise?"

Hannah started twisting her ring. "I don't know."

"Maybe *you* can't forgive yourself."

Hannah recognized the truth of that statement. But it seemed easier to continue beating herself up about it than to believe that she was completely forgiven and let it go. "Maybe the guilt will keep me from messing up again." She stared down at her steamer.

"So you think you're better than God?" Dinah asked.

"What?" Hannah looked up. "Of course not!" She wondered if Aunt Dinah still suffered some side effects from her partying days.

"Well, if a perfect and holy God can forgive your mistakes, then you must have higher standards—"

"That's not what I meant." She paused for a moment, tracing the top of her mug with a fingertip.

"God's love for you doesn't change, no matter how good or bad you are, Hannah." Dinah's words were filled with tender emotion.

"I know." *It's just hard to believe right now*. She knew the verses about God's forgiveness. She knew He took her sins as far as the east is from the west. But it always seemed more true for others than for her. Didn't God expect more from her?

"You'll be okay, Hannah. I'm proud of your stand for purity and what you believe God wants for you—whatever you decide that is. It's okay to struggle. God will make sure you get to the other side safely."

At that moment, Hannah realized she still loved her Aunt Dinah and respected her immensely. "You know what, Aunt Dinah? You're not only my favorite aunt, you're . . . awesome!" Hannah said with complete sincerity.

"Awesome? Those public school kids are really rubbing off on you, aren't they?" She gave Hannah a wink.

• • •

On the drive home, Hannah stared out the window, lost in her own world. She thought about why she believed in courtship and what brought about the uncertainties she had right now. She loved the kisses. She hated the feeling that she was only one of many that Brendan had kissed. She loved feeling special to a guy. She hated worrying that he didn't feel the same way. She loved the giddy feeling she experienced as he skied away that first day. She hated the kick-in-the-stomach feeling she experienced when he walked away the next.

I loved feeling beautiful. I hated feeling insignificant. Can I have one without the other?

• • •

Hannah sat at lunch with the Brio friends, only half involved in the conversation. She was still tired from the night before when she and Aunt Dinah had stayed up late talking. Aunt Dinah left early that morning, showering everyone with hugs and kisses, promising she would return soon and that she would bring Michael. She gave Hannah a long hug.

"Remember what we talked about. I'll be praying for you," she had whispered into Hannah's ear.

She wished her aunt didn't have to leave so soon. There were still so many things she had wanted to talk to her about.

After lunch, the group made their way down the corridor together. It was the week of sex education and Hannah was spending this period in the library. Becca, Solana, Jacie, and Tyler each went to their respective classrooms, shouting plans on where to meet after school.

She twisted around to wave and ran smack into another body.

"Oh, I'm sorry," she said, turning to see who she'd hit.

Brendan's eyes met hers.

"You're back!"

Brendan was on crutches, but he looked pretty healthy in spite of the bandages covering the stitches on the side of his head.

"First day. Like you said—fast recovery." He smiled at her and then became very serious. He said something else, but the bell ringing made his words indecipherable.

Hannah was suddenly aware of his eyes on her, of his body so close to hers. She tensed up, feeling like a cornered puppy desperate for an escape.

"I need to go," she said, dodging around him and sliding through the open library doors. She plunked down into a study carrel and rested her head in her hands.

God, why do I still feel this way?

chapter 20

Hannah woke, startled. Her heart pounded in her chest. *Did I have a nightmare?* She settled back against her pillow.

Thunk! Something hit her window.

What was that?

Thwap!

It sounded like pebbles. Now wide awake, she moved to the window and peered out. A dark, shadowy figure looked up at her. She slid the window open to get a better look. The crutches gave away his identity. *Brendan.*

"What are you doing here?" she whisper-shouted.

"I need to talk to you."

"Shhh," she hushed him, aware that her parents might hear. "What about?"

"Come out here and I'll tell you."

"I can't!" She looked down at her blue flannel nightgown. "I'm in my pajamas. And I can't leave the house now!" The mere idea of sneaking out struck her as completely ridiculous. *What is he thinking?*

"I promise it will only take a minute."

"No. I'll talk to you tomorrow." She shut the window and turned away.

She couldn't believe Brendan was standing outside her window at—her eyes darted toward the red lights of her clock radio—11:47. It seemed surreal—maybe it *was* a dream. *What if he wants to talk more about Christianity? Maybe I should go out there.* Hannah made an agreement with herself. If he was still out there when she looked out the window, she would talk to him.

Thunk! Another rock hit the window before she had the chance to turn around. *Yep, he's still there.*

She opened the window again.

"I'm not going to leave until you come down and talk to me." Brendan's voice gave her chills—more than even the icy air, she noted with a mixture of irritation and pleasure.

"Give me a minute," she said, beginning to close the window. "And get out of the light, please." The last thing she needed was one of her parents or siblings to see him in the front yard.

It's a spur-of-the-moment decision. The only thing I could think to do, she rationalized to herself as she threw on sweatpants and a sweatshirt. She considered pulling her hair back in a ponytail, but with a quick look in the mirror decided to wear it down. *Why am I thinking about stuff like hair at a time like this?* she chastised herself. *I'm as bad as Solana.*

As noiselessly as possible, Hannah made her way down the stairs. Every creak of the step and turn of the doorknob seemed 10 times louder than it ever had before. She tiptoed past her parents' room and heard her dad's soft, even snoring. Her parents would never imagine that she would do something like this. And she didn't know what she'd say if they caught her. She felt like a fugitive, but also oddly excited in this moment of fear and stupidity.

"Hi. Thanks for coming down. I wasn't sure you would." Brendan's deep voice emerged from the shadows as soon as Hannah shut the front door.

"I'm kind of surprised myself," she responded as she tugged her coat on.

"I really needed to talk to you."

"Can we walk out closer to the road?" Hannah looked back toward the large picture window in the house. If someone heard her leave they might come downstairs. And all it would take would be a glance out the window.

"Sure," he said. "Be patient, though. I'm moving kind of slow these days." They walked in silence to the stop sign at the corner.

"Go ahead." Hannah leaned back against a nearby tree and looked up into Brendan's face. Even in the shadows, she could see the perfectly chiseled features and the strong jaw. She sensed his confidence and strength. It was incredibly romantic. Midnight under a full moon, face-to-face with the boy she'd been dreaming about nonstop for over a week, surrounded only by the cool wind blowing music through the trees above them. It seemed too good to be true.

"I'll get to the point, Hannah," he said. His voice was as tender as she remembered it from the ski slope. "I've been thinking about you a lot these last few days."

Hannah's heart did a triple flip.

He went on. "I'm intrigued with you. I haven't been able to get you out of my mind—not since you came into the newspaper office with your pictures."

He paused and then continued as though he wanted to get it all out before he lost his nerve.

"I'd heard stuff about you—about your family and how conservative you are and all, so I tried to stop liking you. But I can't. There's just something about you, Hannah—even beyond the way you look. The kiss we had was different."

Hannah opened her mouth to protest, but Brendan put up a hand to stop her. "I know what I said back then, but it wasn't true. Our kiss was special. *Very* special."

Hannah's heart warmed. *Then kiss me again.* She shook her head, trying to rid it of the wonderful, horrible thought.

"The thing is, Hannah, I'd really like the chance to get to know you better." He balanced on his crutches and took hold of both her hands, looking intently into her eyes. He was so close that she could see the flecks of light brown in his eyes—even in the dark.

"What do you mean . . . how do you want to get to know me better?" Hannah asked, afraid to think of what he was saying.

"I want to date you, Hannah."

"Date?" She could hardly squeak out the word.

"Yeah. I know your parents are anal about the whole idea. But we could do it without them knowing. Like this weekend, you could tell them you're going to the basketball game. Instead, we'd meet at school and go grab dinner somewhere—maybe catch a movie. You'd still get home in time."

Hannah's heart skipped a beat. *Should I?* And then, the answer came to her without hesitation.

"No," she said bluntly. "I mean, no thank you."

His eyes widened. Looking at his face, she realized she was as surprised with her conviction as he was.

"I'm sorry, Brendan. I can't." She released her hands from his and slipped them to her sides.

"Why not? Are you scared of what could happen? Because I know how to do this. You won't get caught."

"No. It's not because I'm scared, or because I don't want to disappoint my parents, or even because it goes against the rules of courtship." Hannah felt her heart surge with the excitement of knowing full well what the truth was.

"Why, then?"

The answer was in the beauty of the night that engulfed them, in the conversation between her and her aunt, and in the way she felt God's love and presence right now. "It's the right decision, Brendan. I believe God wants what's best for me—and you're not it."

"I'm not a bad person. I think I'm good for you," he said, his voice defensive.

She shook her head. "I don't want to hurt you, Brendan. But I deserve more than that. I want a strong, godly man, not just someone everyone thinks is cool and smart."

Brendan looked as though he wanted to speak, but Hannah knew she had to keep talking. She had to make certain she didn't back down. She knew she would melt if she looked into his eyes, so she stared at his nose instead. That wasn't quite as captivating. "I want someone whose heart is purely for me. I don't want to be just another girl—girl number 17 or whatever in your memory bank."

"You wouldn't be. This is different."

"Sure. Right now it seems that way. But in a few days or weeks or months, I won't seem as interesting and challenging. Someone else will catch your eye, and then you'll be after her."

Brendan became defensive. "I'm not promising you the rest of my life. But it would be fun for a while. We're good together. You know that. We had a great time on the slopes."

She was beginning to realize that his nose was pretty cute, too, so she shifted her gaze to his ear. "I want more than a 'great time.' " Hannah matched his tone. "Even though it would be exciting for a while, in the end it would hurt me too much. And that makes it not worth it."

"So you're *sure* you don't want this?" He sounded like the take-charge Brendan she'd known at the newspaper.

"Honestly, I thought I did," she said, trying to hold on to her resolve. She thought for a moment. "I like you a lot. But I'm different than you. I'm different than most of the kids at Stony Brook High. I'm not better than you; I'm just different. I want more than a fun dating relationship with you or any other boy. What I want is something deeper and more committed. That's what's important to me. That's what's best for me."

He stared at her blankly.

"For example, it's really important to me to be with someone who will pursue my heart and be a spiritual leader. Spiritually you and I aren't even in the same book."

"You're right about that."

"I want to do what's best for me, and that means guarding my heart from unnecessary hurts. It means waiting for the right guy no matter how hard or how lonely it gets. I've decided I don't want to get involved with anyone unless I really believe he's the one I will give my heart to—forever. Unless you're ready to do that—" she said, teasing.

"No way!" he said, laughing. He reacted so strongly that he stumbled backward, losing his balance. Before Hannah could steady him, he ended up in a heap on the ground.

"Are you okay?"

Brendan winced, taking in a sharp breath. He sat there for a moment grimacing in pain while attempting to regain his composure. "Yeah, I think I'm all right. At least it keeps my mind off the injured ego." He managed a forced smile.

"Can I help you up?"

"Yeah, just be careful."

Hannah leaned down and tried to give him a boost from his waist. Brendan stood the crutches up and attempted to use them as a hoist to pull himself up. The scenario reminded Hannah of how he had helped her up when she wiped out after getting off the ski lift. Except now the roles were reversed. *In more ways than one*, she thought.

Her weight wasn't evenly distributed, and he was heavier than she. As they tried to struggle up, Hannah ended up falling on top of him. Brendan groaned in pain.

"Oh, sorry. I'm so sorry, Brendan." She tried to move, but her arm was pinned under him. "You need to get up so I can get my arm out."

"If I could get up, we wouldn't be in this situation." He started to laugh—a huge, full laugh. Hannah started laughing, too. There they were, crumpled together, looking up at the stars and laughing.

To Hannah's surprise, she felt strangely free.

"Did you hear something?" asked Brendan suddenly.

Before Hannah could listen, a bright light shone in her face, blinding her.

chapter 21

"What are you kids doing?" The unidentified voice, deep and stern, spoke from behind the light.

Hannah propped herself up from the collapsed pile and lifted her hand to block the spotlight from her face. She couldn't see anything. *This must have been what Saul felt like on the road to Damascus.* Wait . . . there was something . . . blinking blue police lights. Brendan swore under his breath next to her.

Uh-oh. This is not good.

● ● ●

"Thank you, officer." Her dad closed the door behind the retreating policeman. The officer had been relatively nice. He had interrogated her and Brendan before putting them into the patrol car. He had brought her home first, while Brendan waited in the car. The short drive back to the house had seemed like an eternity. A mental slide show of every possible response her father would have played in the forefront of her mind. She couldn't imagine what he would do. And now she was about to find out.

He looked stunned. Still wearing his slippers and wrapped in his terrycloth robe, he settled in behind his desk. Mrs. Connor sat across from him, also with a look of disbelief on her face.

"I don't understand it, Hannah." Mr. Connor shook his head. "This is so unlike you. What happened?"

"I didn't want to . . ." Her voice trailed off. She didn't know where to start or what to say. She didn't understand it herself. It wasn't supposed to happen this way. She had just come to terms with what she believed. It was all falling into place, and now . . . and now, she didn't know how to explain it.

Mr. Connor grew impatient with her silence. "Who was the boy you were with?" Hannah could tell he was trying hard to contain his sternness.

"Brendan Curtis." It came out as a whisper.

"What were you two doing?"

"Nothing. I mean, really, Dad, we were only talking, and Brendan fell backward and I was trying to help him up. He's on crutches because he broke his leg—" As she was explaining, she realized that even though her story was true, it sounded entirely made up.

He stared at her for another minute, his jaw twitching as it clenched and unclenched. She couldn't stand waiting for him to speak. She couldn't bear wondering what thoughts he must be thinking about her—how disappointed he must be. She could see that as well as anger on his face. And why wouldn't he be disappointed and angry? A police officer brings his daughter home in the middle of the night. How shocking is that to a parent?

I have to reassure him.

"Dad, please believe me. Nothing happened. We just had to talk some things out." She knew she must have lost his trust, but she so badly wanted him to know that she was still a good girl.

Mrs. Connor sighed and rubbed her eyes. She put on her mom face—the one that demanded truth, but didn't condemn her. "Hannah, why don't you start from the beginning. I think this whole story started before the ski trip, am I right?"

Hannah nodded. Her mom could always tell things like that.

Mr. Connor leaned forward, giving her his full attention. "It's okay to tell us, Hannah."

In one long rushing paragraph, she told them about the ski trip and the kisses with Brendan and with Tyler and the accident and how awful she felt and how she wanted to make it right.

Hannah took a deep breath when she finished and waited for her parents' response. She realized all their visions of her innocence must be crashing down.

Mr. Connor began to pace back and forth behind his desk. "Well. I *am* surprised. Very surprised."

"Because I failed you?" Hannah asked.

"No." Mr. Connor gripped his desk chair, leaning on it. "Because you have always been so firm in your convictions. We've watched you be sold out to what God wants for you. And once we discussed courtship as the value we've wanted for our family, you've been 100 percent for it."

Hannah bit her lower lip, trying not to cry.

"I'm disappointed with myself," Mrs. Connor told her. "I feel as though we've failed *you*. We should have talked about how boys differ from girls in their thinking and interpretation of situations and the subtle messages sent and received."

Hannah's jaw dropped. "You mean you understand?"

Mrs. Connor moved to put her arm around her daughter. "All too well, I'm afraid. I should have thought to prepare you for something such as this. I guess I didn't think it would ever happen to you."

Mr. Connor moved his chair to sit in front of Hannah. "I'm sorry you didn't think you could talk to us about this. I suppose the situation with Micah had something to do with that."

Hannah nodded.

"But that was different. He's younger. He initiated physical contact that is inappropriate for his age. He was grounded and wasn't supposed to be anywhere but church youth group." Mr. Connor sighed and ran his fingers through his already tousled hair.

"But I was so wrong, Daddy. I messed up."

"Hannah, we all make mistakes as we grow up. We all make mistakes for the rest of our lives. Your mother and I are here to lead and guide you the best we can. Sure, we hope that you won't make mistakes that will hurt you. And we will give consequences for you purposefully disobeying. But that doesn't mean we don't love you."

Hannah looked at the floor.

"I grew up in a family that was very strict and expected perfection. They even rejected your Aunt Dinah for the mistakes she made. Following rules became more important than offering love. I saw what this did to my family, and I knew that wasn't the way God wanted a family to be. So I promised myself to try to find that narrow balance between love and rules. Sometimes that's a balance that's hard for parents to find. Overall, I want love to be more important in this family—no matter how much we mess up."

"I'm sorry," she whispered. "I'm so sorry."

"We forgive you, Hannah," Dad insisted. Her mom nodded in agreement. "Of course, we're disappointed, and your mom and I will have to discuss what we're going to do about it. But never feel like you can do anything that would make us not love you anymore."

The words stuck in Hannah's brain. If Mom and Dad could forgive her—if they could see past her mistakes and love her anyway—then maybe Aunt Dinah was right. Maybe God could, too.

"Hannah, it's late," her mom said, wrapping her bathrobe tighter around herself. "Why don't you go up to bed and we'll talk about this in the morning?"

After exchanging hugs and goodnights, Hannah trudged up the stairs to her room. She sat in her chair and looked out the window. So much had changed that night. What else was going to change?

● ● ●

The next morning she dragged herself out of bed. She'd barely slept, tossing and turning, running all the potential consequences through her mind. She quickly got dressed for school and went downstairs to help her mom.

Mr. Connor met her at the bottom of the stairs. *Strange. He usually leaves for work before now.* He motioned her to come into the den.

"Hannah, your mother and I had a long discussion last night," he began when the two of them were situated side by side on the couch.

Hannah held her breath.

Her dad continued. "We think you should go back to being homeschooled."

"*What?!*" Hannah's heart dropped. Sometime in the early morning she'd settled on the idea that she'd get a lecture and punishment. Maybe she'd be grounded or have to quit the newspaper staff. But she wasn't prepared for this. And she certainly wouldn't have expected her heart to drop the way it did. A month ago she would have rejoiced to hear this decision, but now it seemed the worst possible news.

How ironic, since my life at school has been falling apart. There's that awful tension between me and Tyler. And what about Brendan? Awkwardness at the very least. Rumors about me are probably spreading like wildfire. If I was smart, I'd run. But . . . somehow I need to hold on.

"Dad, please . . ."

"I'm afraid that you're not ready for public school. This environment has obviously had a huge impact on you, and I feel like I'm feeding you to the wolves by sending you there. It's not that I'm angry with you,

Hannah. I just don't know if you have a strong enough foundation to handle the pressures that are going to come your way. I'm afraid I underestimated them." His voice was stern and decisive.

"But Dad, I like Stony Brook."

Her father's eyes met hers. "I'm sorry. I honestly didn't realize it would be this hard for you. But I still think it's what's best. And, as your father, it's my responsibility to keep you from evil. I obviously haven't done that as I should. So today we'll withdraw you from Stony Brook—"

"Today? What about finals? They're only a couple weeks away."

This was all happening too fast. Hannah frantically searched her brain for a way to slow everything down, to somehow go back in time, to figure out a way to stop this horrible moment from ever happening.

"The decision is made, Hannah."

Hannah knew there would be no more arguing.

"Yes, sir." The answer came out in a choke. Trickles of tears made their way down her face.

"Your mother will go in this morning to return your books and do the necessary paperwork." He squeezed her shoulder. "I'm sorry. But we have to do what is best for you."

Hannah knew he wanted to comfort her, but she couldn't accept it. She stared down at the worn carpet and nodded. She couldn't get any words out. Mr. Connor left the den, closing the door behind him, leaving Hannah with her thoughts.

It felt like such a loss. She remembered skiing down the mountain and feeling like she was on a high—doing things she never thought she could do. She remembered taking pictures and then seeing the proofs in the newspaper layout. *Her* pictures—for the whole world to see and appreciate. She remembered teaching class. And even though it hadn't gone quite as well as she had hoped, she had had the opportunity to speak to so many kids—to express her own personal views. And her most precious memories resonated with Jacie, Tyler, Becca, and yes, even Solana. Even if her parents allowed her to continue hanging out with them, it wouldn't be the same. She had grown used to seeing them every day—being a part of something beyond her family. She had done it on her own—made her own friends, become a part of her own group. And now it was all going to be different. She had enjoyed her home-schooled years, and she didn't regret that time. But now she wanted to experience something else—something bigger. Back to the "good ol' days" wasn't going to be good enough.

The wandering tears gave way to full-blown sobs.

• • •

"Hannah, are you okay?" Jacie's concerned voice made Hannah want to burst out crying again, but she bit her lip and attempted to control herself. Jacie had called to see if she could get a ride to school that morning because her car battery had died.

"I'm okay," Hannah said with a squeak, not sure whether she wanted to explain it to Jacie now or not. She feared losing control and sobbing into the phone—the kind of sobs that don't allow words to come out.

"You don't sound it."

Hannah took a deep breath. "I can't go to Stony Brook anymore."

"Hannah . . . oh no . . . why? Is it because of the kisses?"

"Yes and no. I can't go into it right now."

"I'm so sorry."

"It's okay. I mean it's not—but it will be." She tried to sound like she believed it.

"Isn't there anything you can do?"

Hannah knew she would start crying any minute, and she didn't want to explode here—in the middle of the kitchen with her little brothers and sisters all around. "No, there's not. Jacie, I have to go."

"Are you sure? Because—"

"I have to go. I'm sorry. Bye."

As she hung up the phone, Micah stuck his head in the door. "Hey, way to go, Sis!" he said, giving her a two-thumbs up.

"What do you mean?" she responded, her voice hushed.

"I overheard Mom and Dad talking. Sounds like you had quiiiite the night." He grinned. "And all this time I worried you didn't even notice the better gender." He flexed his muscles playfully.

Hannah rolled her eyes. What could she do, deny it? Her only option was to play along. "Watch it or you'll make me lose appreciation again."

"Hey!" he protested, but he stopped flexing. "Seriously, I know what I said the other night, and I'm sorry. And I wanted to let you know—" He swallowed hard, then cleared his throat. "I'm glad you're my sister." He turned and bolted from the room.

• • •

Mom hadn't said much all morning as the two of them got the children ready for the day. Hannah didn't know what she thought of the whole situation.

"I'm going over to Stony Brook." Mom broke the silence as they were cleaning the breakfast dishes. "Would you start everyone on their morning lessons?" The children had already gone to get their books.

"Sure." Hannah had determined that morning she would have a good attitude about being homeschooled. Maybe if her dad saw her reacting maturely, he would allow her to go back to Stony Brook next year. Of course, then it would look like Stony Brook had been the source of all the problems. Hannah sighed. It felt like a lose-lose situation.

Mrs. Connor dried her hands and reached for her coat. "Thank you, Sweetie. I'll be back soon." She walked out the kitchen door and immediately reentered. She went to Hannah and looked into her eyes, searching for a hint of understanding. "Your dad is only concerned about you."

"I know. I just . . ." She stopped, knowing what she wanted to say, but not knowing how to communicate it. "I know, Mom."

Mrs. Connor eased herself down into the kitchen chair. "Dinah did the same thing."

Hannah looked at her. *Aunt Dinah did a lot worse*, she thought, remembering their conversation at the Copperchino.

"She was such a good girl until she turned 16. That was when your dad's parents moved to Columbus. Before that, Dinah had gone to a little country school—a lot of small-town kids. When they moved to the city and she started attending the school there, everything changed."

Hannah hadn't heard this part of the story yet. "Aunt Dinah said she got into a lot of trouble." She leaned against the counter and gave her mom her full attention.

"She told me she talked to you about it." Mrs. Connor nodded. "The thing is, Hannah, when Dinah started making all those bad decisions, it broke your dad's heart. You know how much he adores your aunt. And when he saw her become this completely different person and open herself up to so much pain, it hurt him deeply." Mrs. Connor looked into the distance as she remembered that time. "He's afraid of that happening to you. In the whole scheme of things, what you did wasn't so horrible, but he's remembering Dinah's experience. And he sees it as the first step on a very dangerous path."

Hannah wanted to ask her mom if she agreed with Dad, but she knew her mom would never speak against her dad's decision—no matter how she felt about it. "I understand."

But she didn't really. She wasn't like Dinah had been. Kissing two guys was a bad decision, yes, but that didn't mean she was going to get pregnant. Already she could hear the arguments in her head—arguments she had used when discussing this type of thing with other people. *No one ever starts out thinking they're going to end up going too far. It's like when you put a frog in a pot of water on the stove and turn on the heat. He'll boil to death before he realizes what's happening.* The argument suddenly sounded pretty stupid.

Mrs. Connor stood up, smoothing her skirt. "I'm sorry, Hannah. I know it doesn't seem fair to you, but I hope you make the best of it because that's the way it's going to be." The tone of her voice softened the words.

"Thanks, Mom." Hannah tried to smile.

"I should go. I'll see you in half an hour or so."

Hannah sighed.

And for the rest of my life.

chapter 22

The day went by uneventfully. The other children avoided asking too many questions about why Hannah was there that day. They could tell she was upset. She didn't even have her own lessons yet to keep her mind occupied. *Not like that would help much, anyway*, she thought.

That afternoon, she and her mom went to choose homeschool material for her. Hannah begrudgingly trudged after her mother, attempting to offer an opinion but feeling lead-footed and heavy-hearted. She knew she was dragging, and she could tell Mrs. Connor was trying to be extra patient.

As they pulled the Suburban up to the house, Hannah noticed a strange car in the driveway.

"I wonder who's here," her mom said, articulating Hannah's own thought.

The door to the den was closed, so the two busied themselves making dinner. The excursion had taken longer than they had anticipated, and dinner was already late.

"Do you know who's here?" Mrs. Connor asked Micah as he sauntered into the kitchen.

"Some guy," he said offhandedly, rummaging through the refrigerator. "I didn't recognize him."

Mr. Connor opened the kitchen door. "Hannah, will you please come into the den?" Hannah looked at her mom, hoping to get some clue as to what this meeting was all about, but Mrs. Connor appeared as oblivious as Hannah.

She slowly walked into her father's office and sat across from him at his cherry wood desk. "Yes, sir?"

"I've been bombarded with calls today, Hannah."

"Sir?"

"Jacie, Becca, Tyler, Solana, Kelli, and some others."

"What about?"

"You." He gave her a small smile. "And how you've impacted their lives."

Hannah didn't understand. She had attempted to convert everyone to courtship, yet no one had come to her side of the issue. Instead, she had messed it up. If anything, her impact had been negative.

"In a bad way?"

"No," her dad laughed. "In a good way—in a very good way." He leaned back in his chair. "Each of them told me they've learned from you about having healthier relationships. Even though you may be 'way out there' on some things—I think it was Solana who said that—you've helped shape their thinking into ways that are more godly. And that's commendable."

"Thank you, sir." She felt something strangely like hope rising up in her. Jacie must have spread the word to everyone.

"Even your health teacher called. Ms. Becker?"

"Ms. Bennett. She called?"

"She said she's had a number of girls come in to talk to her about having less physical relationships since you spoke in class."

"Really? That's wonderful!"

"So I decided to call Mr. Curtis."

Uh-oh.

"But he wasn't home," he continued.

Whew.

"Because he was on his way here to see me."

What?

Mr. Connor motioned to the door that Hannah had just come through. In a wooden chair next to it sat Brendan. He gave her a half wave. She had been so confused when she came in that she hadn't even seen him.

Hannah looked back at her dad. The stern look had returned. "Hannah, you did many things in the last week or so that I do not approve of, particularly last night."

"I know."

"But you have also done some things that make me very proud of you."

"Really?"

"Brendan told me about your conversation last night. And even though I still think there was a better way of going about that, your heart was very good."

She couldn't believe this.

He continued. "You're growing up. And I don't necessarily like it. You're thinking on your own. As a dad, I have to admit that scares me. You've made some bad choices." He waved in the direction of the street, as an indication of last night. "But you've also made some good choices. And they've been your own choices. So I'm leaving the decision about where you want to go to school up to you."

"Stony Brook!" Hannah said without a split second of hesitation. She looked up at him. "Really? I can go back to Stony Brook?"

"Yes, but this doesn't mean you're off the hook as far as consequences are concerned."

"Yes, sir." She didn't care. She was beaming.

"And this doesn't mean you can do whatever you want. I still take my role as your protector seriously."

"Yes, sir." And then she added, "And I'm glad you do."

And I mean that.

• • •

Dear God,

I went back to Stony Brook this morning. I've never been so happy to be there. I even had fun in health class. Go figure.

Kelli and Micah aren't dating, but she's allowed to come over to the house and spend time with the family. Mom and Dad seem to like her.

I told Mom and Dad about the roses that I got in Breckenridge. They both think it's sweet but are glad whoever he is hasn't shown up to claim responsibility. They still don't want me to be thinking about boys too much yet. So to calm them down, I recapped how I had questioned courtship but decided to stick with it. And this time it's totally my choice. After all that happened with Brendan, I see how easy it is for me to get emotionally attached to someone—and how much it can hurt. And it's not worth it right now. Dad smiled and said he was glad I had a good head on my shoulders. That felt good to hear.

But I am beginning to see the other side of it, too. Maybe Jacie and Becca were right. Maybe there is an okay way to date, and maybe I was being pretty judgmental because I was so sure my way was best. I know now that courtship is best for me, and I bet for plenty of other girls and guys, too. But maybe it would be better if I encouraged girls to get to know YOU better and to trust You with their future.

Thanks, God, for forgiving me for my mistakes. Thanks for working things out so I could go back to Stony Brook. Thanks for giving me great friends and parents who really care about me. Oh . . . and thanks for teaching me that I can learn as much from my friends as they can from me . . . maybe even more.